My Weekly

2026 ANNUAL

Fiction

COVER IMAGE: SHUTTERSTOCK

Celebrity

Cookery

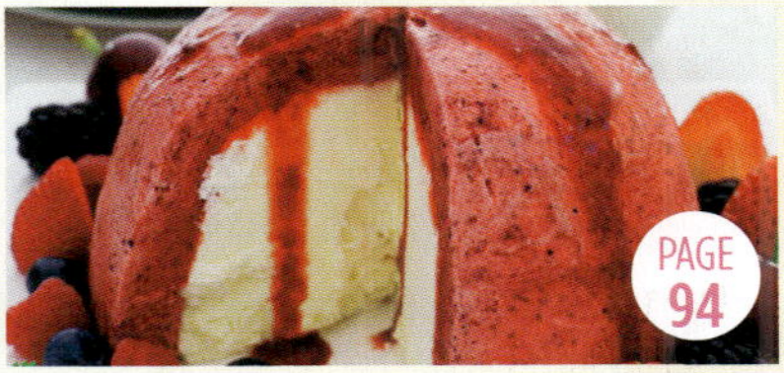

Brainboosters

DC THOMSON

Our Favourite FEELGOOD STARS!

We look at our finest royals, celebrities and personalities who bring warmth, joy and laughter to the nation

Catherine, Princess of Wales

That 2024 proved to be an annus horribilis for the Wales' family is a bit of an understatement. However, the final few months of the year brought a slow and steady return to Kate's public duties as she continued her recovery from cancer, and the nation breathed a collective sigh of relief when we saw her back in the public eye, looking as poised and polished as ever.

Rubbing shoulders with ordinary members of the public is Kate's forte; she has an innate ability to put everyone she meets at ease.

She radiates warmth and goodness wherever she goes and makes us believe that, actually, everything will be okay.

Kate never puts a foot wrong and we love her for that; she's a role model, not only for her wonderful children but for the rest of us, too.

Clearly family-focused, she's a hands-on parent first and foremost. She could, after all, have George, Charlotte and Louis largely brought up by an army of nannies, governesses and assistants but, right from the moment she discovered she was going to become a mother in late 2012, her children have always been her absolute priority – something she herself had instilled in her by her own parents, Carole and Michael Middleton.

Kate said, "They taught me about the importance of qualities like kindness, respect, and honesty, and I realise how central values like these have been to me throughout my life."

While her love of family draws us to Kate, it's the obvious adoration between her and her soulmate William that makes our hearts swell even more.

Our future king is clearly besotted with his wife and the feeling is mutual.

To see them together is as heart-warming as it is life-affirming, and much of that is down to Kate.

Put simply, she manages to make everyone feel good, and long may that continue. ❯

WORDS: SUE DANDO IMAGES: SHUTTERSTOCK, ALAMY

A tough year but still smiling

Good wishes for the princess

A valued member of the Royal Family

Family first for Kate

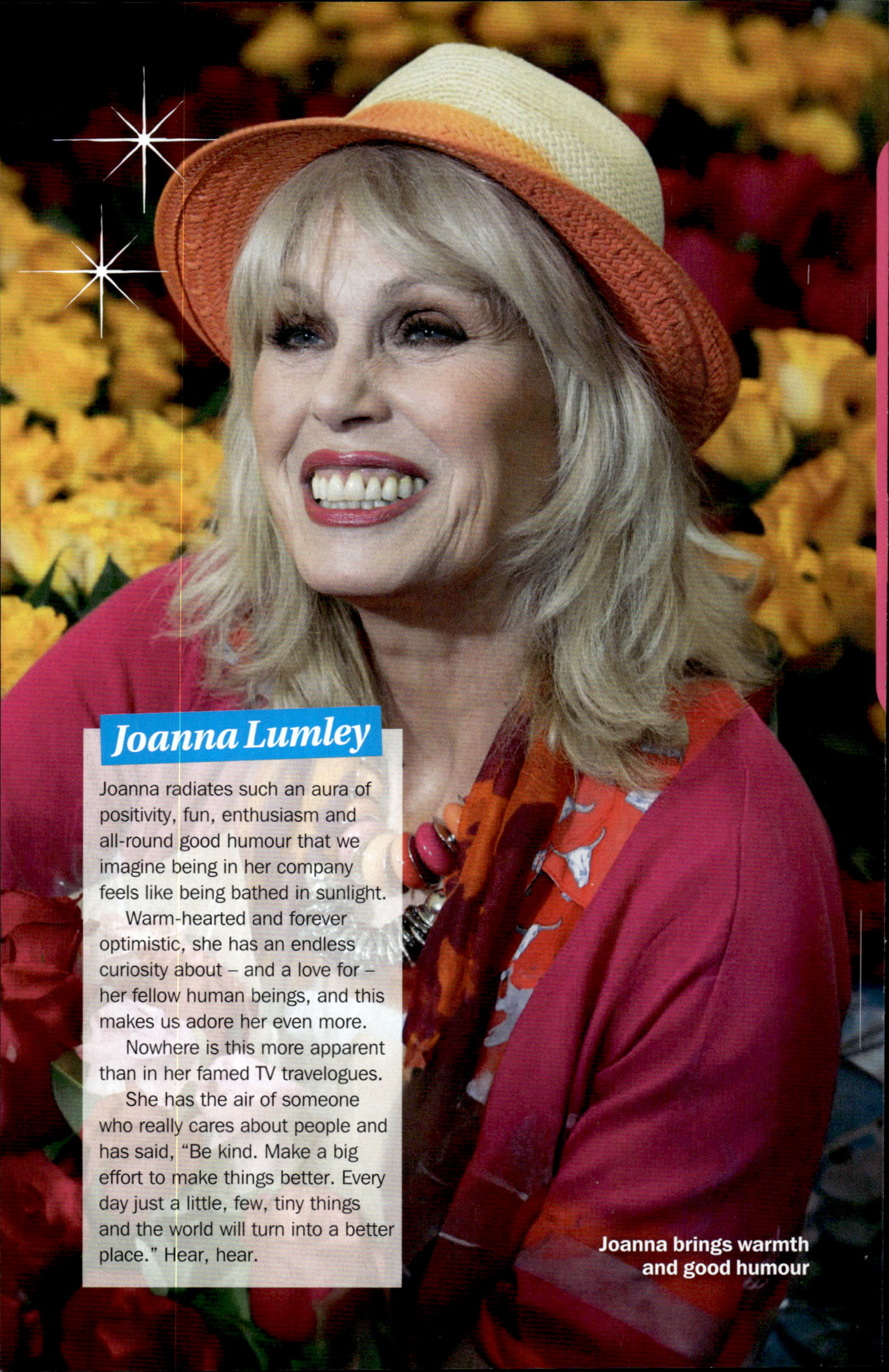

Joanna Lumley

Joanna radiates such an aura of positivity, fun, enthusiasm and all-round good humour that we imagine being in her company feels like being bathed in sunlight.

Warm-hearted and forever optimistic, she has an endless curiosity about – and a love for – her fellow human beings, and this makes us adore her even more.

Nowhere is this more apparent than in her famed TV travelogues.

She has the air of someone who really cares about people and has said, "Be kind. Make a big effort to make things better. Every day just a little, few, tiny things and the world will turn into a better place." Hear, hear.

Joanna brings warmth and good humour

Judi Dench

The irrepressible Dame Judi Dench has a zest for life that has kept her at the top of her game for an incredible seven decades.

Now almost 90, she's known for her elegance, poise and clipped vowels, with an impish sense of humour and a fondness for rude jokes! She even has a rescue parrot, Sweetie, who regularly swears at her, and that's exactly why we love her!

A bit of a rebel, Judi had her first tattoo, "Carpe diem", inscribed on her wrist on her 81st birthday.

Four years ago, she became the oldest woman to feature on the cover of British *Vogue* in the magazine's 104-year history. Bravo Judi!

Josie Gibson

Warm, friendly and funny, Josie Gibson has firmly established herself as one of TVs best-loved presenters, and it's easy to see why.

She's so relatable – just the sort of person we could imaging being best friends with.

Bubbly and genuine with a distinctive Bristolian burr, Josie's natural rapport with people saw her shine on TV for the first time in 2010 when she entered the *Big Brother* house.

She went on to win the show after amassing an incredible 77.5% of the vote. Josie then spent years trying to make her dream of a TV career become a reality.

Her determination is now paying off in spades.

Dignity and poise

Ruth Langsford

While there's been much speculation about Ruth Langsford's thoughts and feelings following her separation from husband Eamonn Holmes, the presenter herself has maintained a dignified silence.

And that's exactly why we warm to the TV regular: her stoicism in the face of extreme adversity puts her high on our list of women we most admire.

A self-confessed homebird, Ruth says, "I'm at my happiest at home in my kitchen. I just like cooking and pottering."

She also insists that family always comes first, making her highly relatable.

We're so full of admiration for this powerhouse of a woman, we could burst with pride at the way she's carried herself in difficult circumstances.

A sense of fun

Michael Ball

Michael Ball is quite simply one of the most popular and well-liked people in showbiz.

He's renowned for his sense of fun and kindness to those around him. A force to be reckoned with, whether it's presenting his show on Radio Two or belting out show tunes onstage with best pal Alfie Boe, Michael also has one of the most rock-solid relationships in showbiz, having lived with his partner, Cathy, since 1992.

A man who emits affability and generosity from every pore, Michael is the kind of guy we feel we could walk up to as a stranger in the street and be confident he'd be charming and lovely – and that's one of the many reasons we adore him.

Olivia Colman

She's one of Hollywood's biggest stars but Olivia Colman's always-smiling face gives off such a friendly vibe we feel like we could easily sit down for a cup of tea and a natter with her.

She began her career in TV comedy (who can forget her star turn in the Channel 4 comedy *Peep Show*?) but has gone on to win numerous awards including an Oscar for *The Favourite*.

At the ceremony she delighted us when she blew a raspberry and stuck up two fingers during her acceptance speech when the powers-that-be tried to cut her off. She was also bleeped out of *This Morning* when she told a very racy joke, although she was so charming and cheeky with it, you couldn't help but laugh.

Comedy moments

Accomplished Women

Had it simply been a night of drinking cheap wine? Or had they achieved something far more worthwhile?

Joanie pushed her largest pair of sunglasses up the bridge of her nose, against her pounding head. Slumping forward, she pressed her forehead against her best friend's pale-pink front door. Was the winter sun always this bright?

Joanie groped around for the doorbell and pushed, wincing at its shrill ring. Right on cue, the noise tipped the miniature Dachshund at her feet into a barking frenzy. Her head swelled with each yap.

Samira flung open the door, recoiling from the light like a vampire in fuchsia silk pyjamas and under-eye masks.

"Best Boxing Night ever," Samira beamed, glancing at the coffee table between them. It was a stained-glass montage of cheap wine bottles, all opened, and all half-drunk.

Joanie nodded enthusiastically, ignoring the hangover bouncing around her head like a pinball. It had been the best night she'd had all year.

There wasn't much competition for this accolade – it had been a tough twelve months. First had come a bitter relationship break-up, although she was now grateful for that.

Gaston was usually the perfect furry little gentleman

"Oh, zip it, you!" she groaned, poking Gaston's nose affectionately with a manicured finger. Gaston wiggled giddily on seeing his second-favourite person.

Samira picked up her "god-dog", tucking him into her dressing gown. She turned and trudged back down the hall muttering, "Why is it so sunny out there?"

Joanie nodded in solidarity with her bestie, as she followed her into her small – and today very offensively pink – flat, flopping onto the sofas.

After a few moments of silence – the comfortable type that only lifelong friends can endure – the exhausted pair managed to manoeuvre their eyeballs to meet each other's gaze, and grinned.

Set up by her deskmate Dave, she would have heeded the red flags . . . if she hadn't already been blinded by Aaron's handsomeness.

Once he had arrived at her flat, twenty minutes late and unapologetic, Aaron had proceeded to drone on about his affluent job and strutted around Joanie's flat in Kermit the Frog socks.

This last offence was too much for Gaston though, who'd had a defiant chew at Aaron's very expensive, very shiny, designer shoes. Gaston was usually the perfect furry little gentleman, and always an impeccable judge of character.

Mortified, Joanie was assuaged into a second date, more out of guilty obligation ›

PICTURES: DCT

than attraction. A tempestuous six-month-long relationship followed, and then quickly withered.

Joanie was more emotionally injured when she was passed over for a promotion at work a few months later, and then physically injured when she tore a ligament at a hockey tournament.

That last misfortune might have been her own fault though – for taking the frustration from her job with her onto the hockey pitch. If only that other player hadn't looked so much like Dave who had set her up, she'd have been able to keep a cool head!

Dave had a lot to answer for this year. However Joanie's cancelled relationship also meant the cancelling of a romantic trip to a Tuscan vineyard.

Once single and emotionally stable again, Joanie had rebooked the trip. She'd planned to celebrate her virtually assured promotion by drinking to her own brilliance. And she was going to use the money from her well-earned rise to pay off the pricey holiday.

When Dave (yes, him again) got the job over her, she graciously shook his hand with her right and cancelled the trip with her left.

She missed her last opportunity to try wine tasting after the hockey tournament.

It would involve a bit of foul play – breaking the "no gift" rule

It was because of this trio of tragic circumstances that it was now late December, and Joanie was yet to complete her New Year's resolution.

This would be the first time in two decades that Joanie would have to disappoint her friend. They prided themselves on being ambitious, accomplished women. Usually when they had a goal, they'd not only score, they'd leave a ball-shaped hole in the net!

This only made the injustice of the missed promotion chafe that much more.

She looked enviously at Gaston, who was now spread across Samira's glittery pink rug, contentedly chewing one of the many Christmas presents she'd bought him. Oh, to be a happy little sausage dog, with no pressures or expectations other than to shake a paw when requested.

Up until this year, Joanie and Samira always achieved their resolutions before the twelve-month deadline. This year's wasn't a particularly introspective or ambitious resolution: *Try wine tasting.* While the rest of the team took a minibus to an upmarket wine bar, she was travelling by taxi to A&E.

Thankfully, Samira was having her own troubles with her resolution: *Paint something I'm proud of.* It wasn't for a lack of trying. Samira was creative and expressive and vibrated with energy.

Yet whenever she painted, her pursuit of perfection took her hostage. So her tiny flat was full of perfectly nice, but perfectly unremarkable, paintings of daffodils and bowls of fruit. There was nothing to be particularly proud of.

If she couldn't resolve her own goal, Joanie could at least help her uninspired friend. But it would involve a bit of foul play – breaking the "no gift" rule.

So, on Boxing Night when the women had their annual get-together, Joanie had rebelliously thrust a wrapped present towards Samira.

Samira wore a peculiar expression of mingled guilt and glee while she greedily tore off the wrapping paper, which was

decorated with pink flamingos in Santa hats. She revealed a miniature set of easels, a pair of canvases and several tubs of cheap poster paints. Samira glanced awkwardly at the expensive equipment she'd invested in that was stashed beside her sofa and offered a faux grateful smile.

Joanie laughed as she explained.

"They're portrait sets! We set them up opposite each other and paint our portraits. They're a popular date night idea at the moment, and while I do love you, Samira –" Samira blew her friend a pouty air kiss –"I got it for another purpose. We're going to tick off your resolution tonight!"

Samira nodded at the bland canvases that lined the walls.

"I love the thought. But how is it going to be any different from this lot? I need to paint something I'm proud of!"

Joanie tapped her nose knowingly.

"I'm absolutely hopeless at anything crafty. So yours is going to be a visionary masterpiece in comparison! You'll just be proud mine doesn't belong to you!"

She laughed a little nervously, worried she'd put too much pressure on her friend, who was uncharacteristically quiet.

Samira disappeared into the kitchen, muttering, "Oh no you don't" to herself.

Horrified, Joanie was about to follow her, when the silky tones of Dean Martin boomed through the tiny flat, waking Gaston from a twitchy dream. He howled along as the spicy intro to *Mambo Italiano* shook the painted daffodils on the walls. Samira emerged from the kitchen clutching three bottles of wine in each hand, a Dachshund-patterned tea towel draped over her forearm.

"Buongiorno, bella signorina," she proclaimed, then added as an aside, "and that is all the Italian I know, so the rest of tonight's performance will be in English . . . with the occasional word pronounced in nonsensical Italiano."

She laid the half dozen bottles across the coffee table and gestured with a dramatic sweep. "I'm not ticking off my resolution without you: If I'm painting something to be proud of, you, signorina, are wine tasting."

Joanie grinned and held her hands up in surrender. This sounded like a good plan . . . and a bad idea.

"Can I interest signorina in a heady bottle of red from the exotic region of ›

Asda? Or maybe a dry Chardonnay from the Arctic fridges of Tesco?" She grinned, twisting off a screw top from a cheap and festive-looking bottle. "Or perhaps a delicate mulled wine from the illustrious cellars of Aldi?"

Ten minutes later, with paints and several glasses of wine set up in neat rows beside them, Gaston asleep again at their feet, Joanie and Samira had raised their brushes, and their glasses.

"Cin cin!"

****

Now here they lay on Samira's velvet sofa, with sore heads and sore faces from laughing so hard.

"Well, we can definitely tick 'try wine tasting' as a completed resolution!"

Joanie grinned, then nodded at the back of the two canvases against the wall. leaning against Joanie, her laughter infectious.

Horrified that her friend's resolution was going to remain unfulfilled despite their best efforts and hangovers, Joanie wiped her eyes and spluttered, "Well, did you paint something you're proud of?"

"Yes!" Samira cried, lifting the dreadful painting onto her mantelpiece.

"What?" Joanie asked, bewildered.

"That's your scrunchie." Samira pointed to a blue blob on the canvas. "That's your dog in your arms. Lap? No, arms! That's your earring . . . I think. Oh, and that's definitely your frown line you get when you're confused – like now!"

Joanie quickly raised her hand to the creased spot between her eyebrows.

"Joanie, I painted YOU. And I'm so proud of you!" Samira grinned and threw her arms around her bemused bestie.

"Without my muse? This is our first gallery showing. I had to wait for you"

"Have you peeped yet?" she asked.

Samira feigned offence.

"Without my muse? This is our first gallery showing, I had to wait for you." The fragile pair heaved themselves from the sofa, and clutched the frames of their canvases sheepishly.

"Ready?"

Joanie braced herself and they spun the canvases around. Gaston yelped and scurried behind the sofa.

A bonkers explosion of colour, bulbous noses, wonky eyes and spiky, neon ponytails were smeared across both canvases. They looked disturbed, preposterous, monstrous!

Joanie held her breath and glanced nervously at her friend . . . who was laughing hysterically.

Samira wheezed and held her side,

This was sweet, and cheesy – distinctively Samira.

"I'm also proud that we managed to paint anything on those canvases in the state we were in last night," Samira mumbled into her friend's hair.

"Two ticks for your resolution then, you over-achiever." Joanie laughed as the friends separated.

Samira nodded at the half dozen half-empty bottles between them.

"Well, if we did a second round of wine tasting, you'd also get another tick." Samira poured the nearest bottle into two clean mugs. "Fancy being an over-achiever too?"

Joanie raised her filled mug.

"To accomplished women."

By Lauren Rebbeck

Brain Boosters

Sudoku

				9				
		3					5	8
	8	6				2		
					9			3
3					2		8	
			7	1				9
		4					6	
	1			6		8	9	
	3		9		1			7

Fill in each of the blank squares with the numbers 1 to 9, so that each row, each column and each 3x3 cell contains all the numbers from 1 to 9.

Turn To Page 171 For Solutions

Word Wheel

You have ten minutes to find as many words as possible using the letters in the wheel. Each word must be three letters or more and contain the central letter. Use each letter once and no plurals, foreign words or proper nouns are allowed. There is at least one nine-letter word.

A Brighter Future

The signs are there, if only we know what to look for. Will a new door open for cynical Becky?

It was a cold, dreary day in January and inside our favourite bistro Dee and I were having our usual Saturday catch-up over a starter and glass of wine.

The Christmas festivities were well and truly over – and so, too, was my relationship with Darryl.

Dee polished her soup spoon and looked at me across the table.

"Did it really matter that Darryl was a vegan?" she enquired.

"Being vegan just isn't for me," I answered. "But quite apart from that, we had nothing in common."

She laughed, and took a mouthful of tomato and basil soup.

"Fair enough."

"Oh, you know what I'm like, Dee. I like walking the dog and going to the cinema and eating out.

I briefly wondered what Darryl might be doing at that moment

"Darryl wanted to book a sky dive, of all things! He said he thought it would be fun to do it together! He loves all that awful active stuff like going to the gym and whatnot. He's quite probably dating Superwoman by now."

"There are plenty of other fish in the sea." Dee giggled and leaned over to top up my glass. Hmm – not heard that one before. "Look, Bec – it's January. I know it can be a bit gloomy, but new year, new start, I say." She took a sip. "Did you know January is named after Janus, the god of doorways?"

"You don't say," I murmured.

"He had two faces, apparently. One faced the past and the other the future. You need to walk through the doorway towards the future and forget Darryl."

I stared at her.

"How do you know all this stuff, Dee?"

"I'm a genius." She shrugged.

****

Once home and snuggled up with my overweight Labrador, I found myself thinking about Dee and her odd but well-meant advice.

"It seems I have to go through a doorway, Bert," I told him. "But first, I have to find a door.

"It's all very confusing, isn't it? You're lucky you're a dog, you know."

Bert licked my hand to show he agreed with every word I was saying. I finished my mug of hot chocolate and briefly wondered what Darryl might be doing at that moment – navigating the ›

PICTURES: DCT

ocean, climbing a mountain, running a marathon? A picture of him in a cloak and tights flashed into my mind and I finally found myself smiling.

****

Monday dawned bleakly, just as raw and cold. The city centre was busy. January meant sales.

It's said that everyone shops online these days, but try telling that to the toy department at Denvers department store. I'd worked there for three years and could never believe the number of toys that were sold after Christmas.

"People just love a bargain," Paul, the manager, commented.

"I refuse to buy anything in January. My bank account doesn't like it," I said.

He laughed.

"OK, I can see you're not convinced. Go and have your break instead."

"Great. Be back in twenty minutes."

****

The restaurant was beautifully warm and smelled of coffee. I bought my cappuccino and made for a table in the corner. Someone else obviously had the same idea and we arrived at exactly the same moment.

"Becky!" he exclaimed. He was smiling, but I had no idea who he was. "Shall we share?"

"If you like."

He was looking at my name badge. I glanced at his.

"Jan?"

He grinned.

"It's pronounced 'Yan'. My mum's Swedish, you see."

Jan, apparently, had just started work at Denvers and already hated the sales as much as I did. I took note of the fact he had fair hair and a very nice smile.

"Twenty minutes isn't long enough to get to know someone, is it?" he said when it was time to leave. He looked embarrassed then. "Actually, I don't know anyone at all yet."

"Everyone's very friendly here," I assured him.

"Yeah, a couple of the lads invited me to the gym, but I'm not really into all that." He flashed that very nice smile. "I don't suppose you fancy meeting for a drink after work later?"

I smiled back.

"I'd like that."

"Thank you, Janus," I said quietly, stepping through the door

We gathered up our things and wandered out of the restaurant together.

"Lift or stairs?" he enquired as we reached them both.

"Definitely lift," I replied.

"Good decision." He pressed the button and the doors slid open. "After you, Becky."

"Thank you, Janus," I said quietly, stepping through the door.

"It's Jan."

"Ah yes, sorry."

"Don't forget that drink. Does seven this evening suit you?"

"Perfect."

The doors closed with a soft click and we soared up to the toy department side by side. I stepped out with a new bounce in my step, and smiled at a giant teddy bear with a reduced price tag on his ear. This was going to be a good day after all.

By Lynda Franklin

Brain Boosters

Codeword

Each letter of the alphabet has been replaced by a number. The numbers for the first name of a celebrity are given. Work out which number represents which letter to reveal the sitcom that Greg Davies created, wrote and starred in.

26	24	24	12	3	5	5		5	24	16	13	7	10	20
	3		3		21		16		7		8		20	
22 G	12 R	3 E	22 G		16	13	15	3	12		6	3	3	9
	1		12		24		7		7		26		1	
20	7	12	3	23	3	6	6		19	7	13	15	12	7
	18		15				16		26				26	
15	3	17	15		7	10	10	26	4	13	15	7	13	15
			3		6				13		12			
11	4	7	18	12	4	24	6	3	15		7	2	7	12
	9				19		26				24		22	
19	4	3	5	6	16		5	9	3	6	3	15	26	13
	6		10		13		16		13		25		13	
19	3	13	4		16	13	13	3	12		16	12	16	5
	6		14		4		22		26		4		5	
24	3	12	14	4	19	3		24	6	4	19	23	3	18

A B C D E F G H I J K L M N O P Q R S T U V W X Y Z

1	2	3 E	4	5	6	7	8	9	10	11	12 R	13
14	15	16	17	18	19	20	21	22 G	23	24	25	26

15	20	3 E

10	6	3 E	7	13	3 E	12 R

Turn To Page 171 For Solutions

Chicken With Grapes

Ingredients (Serves 4)

- **4 x 175g skinless chicken legs**
- **Salt and freshly ground black pepper**
- **Spray cooking oil**
- **2 shallots, peeled and chopped**
- **2 garlic cloves, peeled and crushed**
- **200ml each dry white wine and chicken stock**
- **150g seedless green grapes, halved**
- **1tbsp cornflour, mixed with 2tbsp water**
- **1tbsp freshly chopped tarragon**
- **Oven-baked skinny fries (215cals/100g) and freshly cooked vegetables, to serve**

1 Season the chicken all over. Lightly spray a large non-stick frying pan with oil and heat until hot. Add the chicken legs and cook for 2-3 minutes on each side until lightly browned. Drain on kitchen paper.

2 Add a little more oil. Gently fry shallots and garlic for 5 minutes until softened but not browned. Pour in the wine mix and return the chicken to the pan. Bring to the boil, cover and simmer gently for 25 minutes.

3 Stir in the remaining ingredients and cook gently for a further 5 minutes until cooked through. Serve with fries and vegetables.

RECIPES AND FOOD STYLING: KATHRYN HAWKINS PHOTOGRAPHY: STUART MACGREGOR

The Magic Ring

They seem like a close-knit group, but maybe there is a way in for me . . . even if romance isn't on the cards

LARRY'S RESTAURANT, TWO YEARS AGO.

Is there anything more depressing than the long tail-end of a girls' night out that you never wanted to attend?

Ours is the only table in the restaurant that is still occupied. The lights over the other tables are out. A waiter leans on the bar in the deep shadows of the far corner.

He's a good-looking young man with glossy black hair and a neat beard. Certainly for me, his presence has been the best part of the evening.

While he served us in a smiley and attentive way, I'd repeatedly tried to catch his eye. When our gaze finally met, I wondered whether I'd seen some of my interest reflected.

Clearly feeling sorry for me, Ellen invited me to dinner with her new circle. Feeling sorry for myself, I agreed to go.

I regretted my decision before the starters even arrived. Surrounded by people who knew each other inside out, I felt even more isolated than I would have done if I'd stayed home.

Lilly, Jade, Amelia and Sage really aren't a bad lot, but they aren't my friends – and Ellen shares a life with them that I'm not part of.

They are dressed alike, all sparkly and girly, while I'm shrouded in a black top.

To start, Ellen did her best to include me in the conversation, but my heart simply wasn't in it.

Ellen comes out with the fateful question. "Do you still do your tricks?"

Now, though, I'm fairly sure I must have imagined it. He isn't looking at me. He looks bored, just waiting for the table of excitedly chattering women to finish their coffees and clear off, so he can lock up and go home.

Slumped in my chair, I regard my fellow diners.

Ellen is the only one I really know. She was a good friend at school, but we lost touch when we parted ways for university.

Bumping into her by chance two days ago, I was caught with my guard down and ended up spilling my woes – no job, no man, no plan.

I gradually excluded myself, engaging less and less with any questions directed my way. I let them get on with their merry get-together while I sat on the edge, waiting to go home.

Sneaking a look at the time, I wonder if I should be the one to suggest we call it a night. The restaurant is officially closed.

It's then that Ellen comes out with the fateful question.

"Do you still do your tricks, Pandora?"

"Tricks?" Lilly chimes in, as the others regard me curiously.

"Pandora is a magician!" Ellen declares, proudly, beaming at me.

›

IMAGES: DCT

"Not professionally," I mutter.

"She's so good," Ellen insists. "Go on, Pandora, do that one where you draw what someone else has drawn without you seeing it."

"Ooh, I've seen that on telly," Amelia joins in. "Can you really do that?"

"Do it on me," pleads Ellen, eyes wide.

"I can't do it on you," I smile. "Jade will think you're an accomplice."

"Try it on me," challenges Jade, the group's cynic, leaning forward.

I'm tempted, because there's no way she could cheat and make it look like it hasn't worked.

But I have a better plan: a chance to impress the handsome waiter.

I don't want to draw attention to his distress. The others haven't noticed

"We need someone none of us knows," I say. "Excuse me, waiter?"

He brightens as he comes over and I dare to hope it's because he likes me.

"Are you ready for the bill, ladies?" he asks hopefully.

Maybe I read his eagerness wrong.

"Well, yes, soon, but first I want to see whether I can read your mind."

"You won't find much to read in mine," he quips with a wry look.

"Toby, isn't it?" I ask.

"How did she know his name?" Ellen whispers, agog.

"He introduced himself when we arrived," Jade says dryly.

I ask Toby if he has his order pad and pen and he holds them up.

"Would you mind tearing off a couple of blank pages and handing them to me?" I ask him.

He passes them over and I put them on the table to the right of my plate.

"In a second I'm going to turn away," I continue, "and, without me seeing, I want you to draw a very simple picture on your pad. Just a drawing of a dog, or a house, or a tree – anything you could sum up in one word."

"OK."

I turn away and shield my eyes so I can't see him drawing.

"Done?" I turn back. "Now, hand me the pad, face down, low to the table."

Our fingers touch as I take it. Tingling, I wonder if his drawing is a flirty message – or a sign he's unavailable.

"I'm putting it here, to the left of my plate," I continue, "and I want you, Lilly, to put your hand on it to make quite sure that it doesn't move.

"Toby, can I borrow your pen?"

I hold the pen solemnly.

"This will be helpful, because it's coated in your psychic energy."

"Oh, for goodness' sake," Jade murmurs, rolling her eyes.

"What I want you to do now, Toby, is picture your drawing as vividly as you can while I reproduce it on this page."

With every eye on me, I hold the pen over the paper. I close my eyes and tilt my head, a slight crease in my brow as if trying to receive a telepathic message.

"You've drawn something unusual for a man." I put a finger to my temple. "I'm getting something symbolic."

Toby's unsmiling face reddens.

"What is it?" Ellen cuts in, eagerly.

"It's something expensive," I go on. "But I'm getting the feeling it's not the price that makes this object valuable. It's the strong emotions attached to it . . ."

I look up into his face, hoping that I might see a flirty smile.

Instead, I realise I've wandered into an area I shouldn't have.

"Strong negative emotions?" I croak, before I can stop myself. Not liking the turn this has taken, I decide to wrap it up.

I quickly draw two big circles, one inside the other, and a small circle on top, with lines radiating from it.

I hold it up.

"Is this the ring you drew?"

Toby nods, grimly.

The others might have taken his silent answer for shock at my mind-reading ability, but I can see the pain in his eyes and it hurts me deeply.

"Lilly," I say, forcing a smile. "Show us what he drew."

Lilly turns over the pad and everyone gasps and claps at the sight of Toby's drawing: a diamond ring identical to the one I sketched.

"Is that all you need from me?" says Toby. "Only, I've got to . . ."

He gestures over his shoulder as if he's needed elsewhere. Before he hurries away, I glimpse the tears in his eyes.

I yearn to go after him, but I don't want to draw attention to his distress. The others haven't noticed.

"I have to admit I don't know how you did that," Jade confesses.

I smile thinly, but feel no smugness, just guilt for accidentally upsetting a man I've had my eye on all evening.

What could be so bad about a ring? I wonder. And if so, why draw it?

"Do another trick," Ellen urges. "Make something disappear."

"No, no, it's getting late," I demur. "I think they've been waiting to close for about half an hour."

"Actually, yes, we'd better make a move," Sage agrees.

There's a hubbub of parting chat as we pay our share of the bill and get up to leave. Toby has regained his professional smile as he helps us into our coats and scarves at the door.

I long to make amends to him – but not in front of everyone else.

I wait until we are a little way along the pavement, with everyone talking about rides home and plans for their next meet-up.

"Oh, I'll just take this back." I hold up the waiter's pad that I pocketed earlier. The others don't even see me slip away.

****

Toby has bolted the door, but opens it when I tap on the glass.

"This is yours."

"Thanks." He beams in a way that makes my heart skip. "I didn't say it earlier, but your trick was amazing."

I bask for a moment in the admiration of his warm brown eyes.

"I really didn't mean to upset you, though," I say softly.

"My own fault." He shrugs. "I should have drawn a cat or a dog. Somehow, I'd drawn the ring before I realised."

"Because it was on your mind?" I prompt him gently.

Toby heaves a sigh and sags against the doorframe.

"I offered the ring to someone last night – I proposed – and she didn't accept. She doesn't want to marry me."

"Oh no, I'm sorry."

He takes a red velvet box from his pocket and opens it. The streetlights glint on the real-life version of his drawing.

"I'm still carrying it around with me like an idiot," he says.

"It's beautiful," I breathe, and can't help thinking, *I wouldn't have said no if you'd offered that to me.*

"Maybe she'll come around?" I try to console him.

He shakes his head.

"All the while I was working up the ›

courage to propose, it turns out she'd been wondering how she was going to break up with me. As it happened, we both told each other on the same night. It's over. That's it."

"Are you going to be on your own tomorrow?" I ask gently. Tomorrow is Sunday, and I know what a lonely Sunday can feel like after a break-up.

"No, I'm going to my parents'," he says briskly. "Big family get-together. That should take my mind off it."

"Can I take your number?" I venture. "Maybe give you a call to . . . er . . . make sure you're all right?"

"Um... I guess." His reluctant tone stings like a rejection.

It's not every day that I make the first move. It's actually my first time, and I couldn't feel more embarrassed by his lack of enthusiasm.

I tell myself he isn't really giving me the cold shoulder, it's just too soon after his rejection to be thinking about meeting someone new.

Cursing my social ineptness, I wish I could make myself disappear.

Thankfully, he takes out his phone and we swap details, albeit awkwardly.

"I can do another mind-reading trick over the phone for you," I say with slightly forced brightness.

"Do you know what I'd really like?" he asks. "If you'd tell me how you knew what I'd drawn tonight."

"Maybe one day I'll tell you," I tease.

He rewards my air of mystery with a genuine smile.

On the way home I wonder if my magic will win him over, or whether I have just made a complete fool of myself.

LARRY'S RESTAURANT, LAST YEAR.

The restaurant is packed and buzzing with cheery conversation as I pull a chair up to the end of a table for four.

"Evening, guys. I'm Pandora. May I show you something magical?"

I toss a coin from left hand to right, and then I show them both of my hands, front and back, to reveal that the coin has vanished.

I've loved magic since I was seven years old, when my grandad showed me an empty hand and then appeared to pull a ten pence piece out of my ear.

It was the only illusion he knew, but after I'd begged him to show me how it was done, he bought me a book of magic tricks for my birthday.

Before long I was astounding my school friends by getting them to pick a card, then making it disappear from the deck and reappear between the pages of a book on the far side of the classroom.

Even the teachers were baffled.

I guess, despite being otherwise shy and introverted, this newfound ability to impress went to my head.

Addicted to those awestruck reactions, I spent every spare hour practising card manipulation – covertly moving a particular card around a deck with my fingers as I fanned, shuffled and cut it – until whatever card a person picked, they always ended up with the one I chose.

As slick as I became, I never dreamed that I'd ever be able to turn my party tricks into a living.

In fact, after I left university with no degree, just a mountain of student debt, I wondered if I'd ever make a living at all.

Without a gang of school or uni friends to impress, I began to think that all those hours I'd spent alone in front of a mirror making things vanish and reappear had been a waste of time.

How dramatically things have changed since I met Toby.

After he persuaded his boss to let me entertain his customers as a table magician, life has picked up in ways that ›

still amaze me. Word got around and before long I was being booked for private parties, corporate events and stage shows.

Leaving a table full of happily mystified diners, and sashaying to the next, I pass Toby who is carrying an armful of used plates towards the kitchen.

As we squeeze past each other, we exchange a wink.

Perhaps my magic is working on him. Or maybe his is working on me.

Either way, life feels decidedly magical.

LARRY'S RESTAURANT, THIS YEAR.

With the restaurant buzzing around us, I sit at a table opposite Toby. It's a rare evening off for both of us and we're dressed to the nines, him looking more gorgeous than ever.

"It's two years to the day since you did that drawing trick on the evening we met," Toby says with a grin. "Will you do it again for me tonight?"

"Seriously?" I laugh.

"Please, it will mean a lot." He has his order pad and pen in hand.

"Go on, then." I dutifully turn away and shield my eyes while he draws.

Taking the face-down pad, I put it on the table to the left of my plate.

"Is there a reason you've drawn the ring again?" I tease.

"How do you know that?" Toby asks in astonishment.

I tap my forehead.

"Mind-reader, remember?"

"Really, though," he insists, "how do you do it?"

"Hand it to me again and see if you can spot what I do."

He passes the pad to me and I put it to the left of my plate.

Toby shakes his head.

"I didn't see anything."

"Once more, in slow motion. Now watch carefully. As I pass the pad over my plate, I can see the reflection of your drawing in the blade of my knife."

"It's as simple as that?" He laughs.

"Well, that and the fact that you've got 'ring' almost printed on your forehead, because of the one burning a hole in your jacket pocket."

Toby's mouth drops open.

"How could you possibly...?"

"I saw you put it there earlier," I laugh, "and you keep putting your hand on it to check it hasn't disappeared."

"Well, I guess you got me," he chuckles, red-faced.

Bringing out the red velvet box, he turns it nervously in his hands and butterflies flutter in my stomach.

"When you told me this was too beautiful to take back to the shop," he begins, "I dared to hope you meant that one day you might like to wear it."

"Is this a proposal?" I enquire, my heart quickening.

He opens the box and the colour disappears from his face.

"Where's the ring?" he demands in horror. "It was in there . . . and it's gone!"

"What, this ring?" I waggle my fingers to show that I'm already wearing it.

"It looks like a perfect fit," Toby says, shaking his head in amazement.

"That's because I had the size adjusted last week."

"You mean you knew I was going to propose tonight?"

"Let's just say I hoped you might! And take that as a yes."

He takes my hand in both of his and kisses my fingers. I gaze at the sparkling diamond and can't help thinking that there was definitely something magical and mysterious about the way that ring brought us together.

By Julia Douglas

Moroccan Chicken and Orange Salad

Ingredients (Serves 2)

- **100g couscous or bulgur wheat**
- **1tsp stock powder (or ½ stock cube)**
- **400g can chickpeas, rinsed and drained**
- **2 small handfuls baby spinach**
- **1 small carrot, grated**
- **½ small red onion, chopped**
- **40g sultanas or raisins**
- **1 large orange**
- **2 roast chicken breasts, skin removed**
- **1tsp ras-el-hanout seasoning**
- **A few mint sprigs, to garnish**

For the dressing

- **2tbsp olive oil**
- **1tbsp orange juice**
- **½tsp Dijon mustard**
- **1tsp clear honey**
- **Salt and pepper**

1 Cook the couscous or bulgur wheat according to pack instructions, adding the stock powder or cube to the cooking water. When cooked, rinse with cold water and drain well. Mix with the chickpeas, then share between 2 serving plates with the spinach, grated carrot, red onion and sultanas or raisins.

2 Using a sharp serrated knife, peel the orange, removing all the peel and pith. Cut into segments, removing all the membrane. Divide between the salad plates.

3 Tear the roast chicken into bite sized pieces, then arrange on the salads. Sprinkle with the ras-el-hanout seasoning.

4 Make the dressing by mixing together the olive oil, orange juice, mustard and honey. Season. Serve the salads, drizzled with the dressing and garnished with mint leaves.

RECIPES AND FOOD STYLING: SUE ASHWORTH
FOOD PHOTOGRAPHY: JONATHAN SHORT

The Boat Library

The village had waited a long time for this project to come to fruition. How would residents react when disaster struck?

Marion clasped her hands together as she rose to her feet to address the rows of residents in front of her.

"Apologies for the lack of village meetings over the past couple of months, but thank you all for coming this evening."

Ripples of applause vibrated around the cold community hall. Hats and scarves remained firmly in place.

"Well, I have some very exciting news for you all today."

She paused, hoping her announcement would deter the couple at the back from scrolling on their phones.

"The commission for the boat library has been completed!"

Marion beamed with so much pride, it was as if she had created the masterpiece herself.

When the photographs were finally returned to her and the murmuring subsided, she continued.

"It should be put in place sometime in the next couple of weeks. It's on wheels for easy transportation, but John will secure it to the flagpole."

"How will it work, Marion? Will there be a key, or designated people in charge?"

Marion looked into the crowd, addressing the man who had spoken.

"That's not really how a community library works, Mr Edgley.

"How are we going to stop folk taking but not replacing them?"

"At last!" someone shouted.

Cheers erupted.

Marion smiled into the crowd.

"And the council have given their permission for it to be located on the square at the start of the prom. This will be an ideal position, being right on the junction between Sandy Ridge and the beach road."

Marion cast her eyes to the folder she'd placed on the table in front of her and shuffled through its contents.

"John, the carpenter who kindly gave up his time to create this beautiful addition to the village, has sent over these photos for us all to admire!"

She handed them to the nearest resident who duly passed them on.

"This has been designed so that people can bring their old or unwanted books to the boat library and help themselves to any other book in there.

"As you can see from the pictures, it has two sturdy glass doors on the front, but anyone can open them." She held up one of the photos and pointed.

"We're hoping the locals will keep the library well stocked, but of course, tourists are more than welcome to use it. We'd appreciate donations from anyone, providing the books are in reasonable condition, of course."

"How are we going to stop folk taking but not replacing then?"

Jim Dyers was on his feet, pointing a wagging finger at Marion.

›

PICTURES: DCT

Marion sighed as quietly as she could, sucking in a deep breath before speaking. Jim was at every meeting and always had a moan about any suggestion or solution to issues raised.

"This is going to be a community library, Jim. There is no pressure on people to put books in simply because they have taken some out."

Jim slumped to his seat, muttering, "How's that going to work? What if folk only take out and don't put back? Boat will be empty before we know it."

"And what folk exactly would you be referring to, Jim?" Lena from the post office piped up from two rows behind.

"I thought we could use the bottom shelf for children's books"

"Not me, that's for sure!" Jim tapped his chest for emphasis.

Marion interjected before the conversation got heated.

"Well, why don't we just give it a go before we start discussing problems that may never occur."

There was a break for coffee, tea, and slices of Madeira or lemon drizzle cake kindly donated by Cakes by the Sea.

The meeting resumed and other topics were discussed, but the conversation kept returning to the boat library. It had been in the planning for well over a year and the residents were excited to see the plans eventually coming together.

"So if we want to donate but the boat is full, what can we do?" Mrs James from The Strand queried.

"Good point, Mrs James. If you could possibly hold on to them until there's space on the boat, then that would be much appreciated."

Marion closed the gathering by letting everyone know when the next meeting was to be, adding that she hoped by then the boat library would be in place and they could discuss how things were going.

****

Marion was going to meet up with John ten days later. He'd emailed to say that he was bringing the boat library over on his trailer.

She'd only ever communicated with John via email or over the phone and was looking forward to meeting him in person. She'd broached her idea of a community library with him, and it was he who had come up with the charming idea of it being in the shape of a rowing boat.

Apt for this village, he had concluded.

With the summer season long over, only a straggling handful of tourists roamed the prom. The weather had shown signs of storms and the high tides had already caused some damage around the promenade.

There he was! She hurried over, using one hand to hold onto her hood and holding out the other one to John.

"Wow, John. It looks even better in real life. It's marvellous! It must have taken some work to get it looking this good."

John waved a dismissive hand.

"It was nothing."

She took off her glove and ran her hand down the varnished wood. Two oars were fastened to the side of the "boat which stood about six-and-a-half feet high. She opened the doors and peered in. Five deep shelves were slotted inside, with a taller space at the bottom.

"I thought we could use the bottom shelf for children's books. They're always a bit bigger, aren't they?" John suggested.

Marion stepped back and beamed.

"I hadn't given a thought to children's books, John. What a wonderful idea. Children will love it; I know my two granddaughters will be sorting out their books as soon as they know."

"Why do you think I suggested it?" John smiled. "Fancy a coffee? Just to go over the finer details."

Marion slipped her hand into her bag.

"That would be grand, but I've got to be the first to deposit a book."

She placed a copy of a World War Two saga written by one of her favourite authors on the middle shelf. There came a hearty laugh from John behind her.

She swung round.

"Great minds," he explained, as he lifted a rather battered-looking crime novel from his work bag and placed it next to her book.

"Let's grab that coffee," she said, and they made their way to The Cwtch.

****

The following month's meeting had an important agenda of dog fouling that unfortunately could no longer be blamed on the tourists, so people were keen to discuss solutions.

Marion raised her hand, trying to get some order around the room.

"I think we can now move on to discuss the success of the boat library." She smiled broadly. "I'd like to thank everyone for their contributions. Since the boat library has been in place, it has been full of books. The children's section has been widely appreciated."

"I picked up five books I haven't read yesterday, Marion. It's a pleasure to have it in our community," Mrs Oates said, the delight evident in her smile.

"I put five back too," she added quickly, glancing over at Jim.

"That's lovely to hear, Jean. It seems it's achieving its purpose. There have been a few hiccups, but . . ." She scoured the room and spotted the carpenter's friendly face. "John has been at hand to fix any problems. So thank you, John."

He nodded and smiled in her direction.

****

Marion made a point of visiting the library once a week, just to check if she needed to make more appeals for books and to sort through its content. She'd come across one or two she'd deemed inappropriate for the public eye.

After stacking the children's books on the bottom shelf, she glanced up. The clouds were thickening and racing across the sky. The prediction of Storm Agnes looked likely to be fulfilled, and Marion wanted to get home before the blustery wind started whipping the sand up from the beach.

As she reached her house, the thick, fat raindrops began to fall and her cosy log burner was a welcome sight.

****

As the howling wind roared, Marion's sleep was restless. She dozed lightly and the sound of her phone mingled with her dreams. She almost missed the call. Glancing at the screen, she saw that the time read 6.40am.

She sat up quickly, now fully alert. This was too early for a general chat.

"Hello?"

"Marion, it's Doreen."

Doreen was a neighbour who often relied on Marion to pick up a bit of shopping for her, but even Doreen didn't usually call this early.

Marion swung her legs over the side of the bed and felt around for her slippers.

"Everything OK, Dor?"

"Have you looked outside this morning?" her neighbour asked. ›

"Um, no. I was still in bed," she said as she headed for the window. "What am I looking for?"

"You'll see," came the quick reply.

Marion pulled back the net curtains and she gasped.

"Oh, my goodness. What on earth?"

"Jen just called me. Sandy Ridge, Cold Road and The Strand are all the same."

"Let me get dressed. I'll head down straight away."

Marion ended the call and dressed as quickly as she could. The wind was still fierce, but the rain had eased.

She hurried down the hallway and as soon as she opened the door, some of the debris strewn around her garden blew into her hall. Pages and pages of wet, soggy words stuck to her wooden floor.

She pulled the door closed behind her and hurried down the street.

John dropped to his knees, checking the doors, which seemed at least intact.

"The wind must have pulled the doors open. I'm afraid I underestimated the ferocity of a seaside storm."

Marion laid her hand on his shoulder.

"It's not your fault, John. No one could have predicted this. We haven't had a storm this bad in a long time."

John stood up.

"I'll fetch the trailer, get this back to my workshop. I'll get it dried out and assess the damage. It could probably do with some stronger hinges, but . . ." His eyes scanned the roads and gardens around them, pages fluttering down and gathering like seagulls. "What are we going to do about all this? Folk aren't going to be too pleased."

"Don't you worry about that. You get the boat sorted and I'll see to the rest."

"I'm afraid I underestimated the ferocity of a seaside storm"

Every garden was the same. She stooped to pick up a bedraggled copy of a rom-com marooned in a muddy puddle. How had this happened?

She retrieved her mobile from her bag and scrolled to John's name.

"John? I'm really sorry to call you so early, it's just that –"

"I know. Luke just called me, I'm on my way. Meet me there?"

Marion raced to the prom. Everywhere she looked there were remnants of paperbacks. Loose pages swirled around her feet, lifting into the air before dropping back to the ground.

She could see the glass doors swinging in the wind as she neared the boat library. John's van was just pulling up.

"Oh, John. Look, it's completely empty," she wailed.

She waved as John's van disappeared down Sandy Ridge, then fired off a quick message to the village WhatsApp group.

I'm sure a lot of you are aware of the mishap with the boat library in the storm last night. John has already collected it to fix it, but I'm going to need your help with the clean-up if anyone is free.

As soon as the message was sent, her phone began to ping with responses.

She bought black bin bags from the local shop and started on the dispiriting task of collecting wet pages hanging off branches and clogging drains.

Soon a crowd had arrived, and bags were handed out.

"It's such a shame. All these books ruined," Marion said, her voice breaking with the build-up of emotion.

Mrs James patted her back. ›

"Look – some of them might be salvageable," she said, holding up a dripping Agatha Christie classic.

Marion took the book from her.

"I love your optimism, Mrs James!" she said as a grin developed on her face. And she realised that all was not lost.

The support was overwhelming. Marion heard no words of complaint, not even from Jim.

"We've enough people in this community to get that boat library full again," he'd said gruffly as he shuffled along with his litter picker.

"Thanks, Jim."

****

By the end of the day, the village had reverted to its normal state, cleared of flying books and rogue pages. Marion was exhausted, but the feeling of community spirit lifted her mood.

She called John.

"It was amazing, seeing the community come together," she told him. "I'm sure once the boat library is back in place we'll fill it again pretty soon."

"I've no doubt about that! My grandson has already sorted out his donations and Brenda next door has brought a box around, although you might want to vet some of her choice reading material!"

Marion heard the amusement in his voice and was touched by the way John always brought a smile to her face.

"That's good to hear. I will definitely give them a once-over! I'm afraid to ask about the damage. Can you fix it?"

"On closer examination the doors are a write-off, I'm afraid."

"Oh, that's such a shame," Marion said, her shoulders slumping as she dropped to the sofa.

"But never fear, it's nothing that can't be sorted. I've ordered new doors with toughened glass and stronger hinges. I'm also looking at a latch system, one that hopefully won't be damaged by any storm that gets thrown at us in the future."

"Oh, that's marvellous, John. I can't thank you enough."

"It's what this village is about, Marion – and the reason I never have any intention of leaving here."

****

Marion was looking forward to chairing the next village meeting. The agenda was full, but the boat library took top priority.

"I can't thank everyone enough for their help and support with the boat library disaster!" she said warmly. "When I saw the streets paved with pages of Sherlock Holmes and murder mysteries I envisaged a fracas. What I got was overwhelming support. So thank you, everyone – you have all shown how much our community means to us."

She paused to let applause die down before carrying on.

"And a huge thanks to John, who repaired our boat library and got it back to where it belongs. The new book donations have been staggering and the boat is once again full to bursting.

"I've always known this village was a good place to be and since this venture, I've met people who have lived here as long as I have, but whose path I have never previously crossed."

She cast her gaze to the back of the room. A wink greeted her and she smiled.

"And for those people, I will always be truly grateful."

She swallowed the lump rising in her throat and folded the paper before pulling her steel-framed glasses off by the arm.

"Now, let's all celebrate the outstanding success of our relaunched boat library with coffee and cake!"

By Christina Collins

Brain Boosters

Kriss Kross

Try to fit all of the listed words back into the grid.

4 letters
CRAW
HYPE
NOVA
OBEY

5 letters
BESOM
OCHRE
TENET
TOWEL

6 letters
ALLEGE
BIOPSY
EPONYM
GHETTO
OCELOT
SEPTUM

7 letters
OVERSEE
PROVISO
SECLUDE
TEENAGE

8 letters
ECSTATIC
IDLENESS
NAUTICAL
SYMMETRY

13 letters
HYDROELECTRIC
SUPERNUMERARY

Turn To Page 171 For Solutions

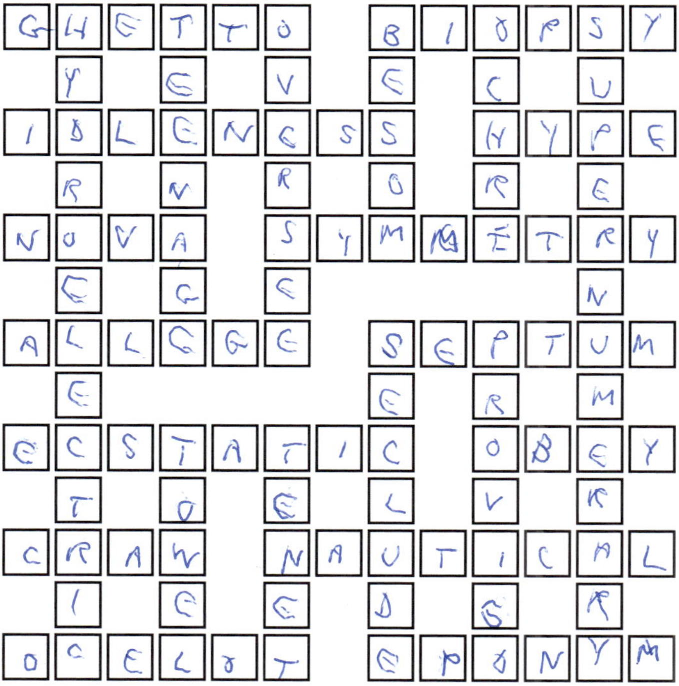

The Science Of Attraction

The heady worlds of physics and astronomy are closed to a mere girl – but romance may be another matter . . .

WOOLSTHORPE MANOR, 1666

"Look up!" Sarah Beckett pointed to the cloudless sky. "See the moon, Mary."

The sun was behind Sarah, warming her back as she walked. And there hung the beautiful silvery moon just above the trees ahead. She wished she really understood quite what it was.

Her father's books gave some explanations, of course, but the concepts felt obscure to her. She carried some of her own ideas with her now, about the moon's movement across the heavens, her neat handwriting on the rough papers interspersed with the occasional diagram.

"You do not often see the moon in daylight." Sarah poked her sister in the shoulder. "Look."

Mary glanced up briefly, managing to convey more with her indifferent shrug than any number of words.

Mary was only eleven, more interested in farm animals than in the way the world worked. Sarah was nineteen and could not think of anything more wonderful to be than a natural philosopher like Isaac.

Yet what chance did she have? A mere woman? Unless Isaac would . . .

"Freddie!" Mary started running. Freddie was waving by the house. His dog, Jack, was at his side.

Sarah sighed as her sister ruffled Jack's ears and allowed him to put his paws against her dress. She'd had words before from her mother for returning Mary home with a dirty dress, a bloodied knee or a scuffed elbow.

But what could Sarah do? Mary was so full of life. There wasn't a tree in the village she hadn't climbed – or fallen from – and not one stream she hadn't jumped across, or fallen into.

"You are wasting your time, my dear. You do know that?"

She returned to kicking a stone along the path towards Mr Newton's house.

"Will Freddie be there today?" she enquired hopefully.

"Let us hope so," Sarah answered.

If Freddie – son of one of Woolsthorpe Manor's groundsmen – was around, then Sarah would be able to speak to Isaac alone while Mary played with her friend.

"Morning, Miss Sarah." Freddie doffed an imaginary cap.

"Good morning Freddie. How are you?"

"Just grand, Miss Sarah, ta very gladly." He pointed to the big house. "Mistress Hannah's in the kitchen, if you're lookin' for 'er."

"Thank you, Freddie."

Sarah had not really come to see ›

PICTURES: DCT

Isaac's mother, however. She wished to see Isaac himself.

Sarah and Freddie walked away, whispering and giggling, Jack padding along beside them.

"We'll be leaving soon, Mary," Sarah called after them. "Mother wants me to go the village to –"

But they were gone already, round the back of the house, planning on getting up to who knew what.

Sarah headed for the kitchen, knocking at the open door.

"Good morning!"

The heady aroma of cakes baking made her stomach growl.

Hannah, Isaac's mother, was sitting at the kitchen table, writing in a book.

"Sarah Beckett! How lovely to see you. Are you well? Your parents?"

"All very well, thank you. And you?"

"Frustrated. Annoyed. Desperate for any distraction to take me away from these pestilent books." She gestured at the pages filled with columns of figures. "You'd think with Isaac's talent for numbers, he could at least spare a little of his time to help with the household accounts. But no, he's always off somewhere, thinking those grand thoughts of his." She glanced at the papers in Sarah's hand. "Is it Isaac you are here to see?"

"If he has time. I do not want to intrude, though."

Hannah smiled. "You never intrude, Sarah. In fact, I wish Isaac would spend less time with his science and more time with . . ." She shook her head, as only a mother can. "Well, you know Isaac."

Sarah recognised the weary exasperation Hannah displayed. She had seen it enough in her own mother.

"So is he around? Isaac? I have something new I wish to show to him."

"You are wasting your time, my dear. You do know that? You might be able to hold Isaac's interest for a while, when you give him a puzzle to solve, but then . . ."

"I am looking for nothing more than help with my scientific investigations."

Sarah knew her cheeks were flushing.

"Science is no pursuit for a lady," Hannah said flatly. "You will never be accepted. Your voice will never be heard."

"But I –"

"This is a man's world, Sarah. No matter how hard you try, you cannot make it otherwise.

"And if you persist in these follies you may lose your chance for happiness, for a good marriage. Peter in the village is always happy to see you. You would do better to allow him to . . ."

"Peter is lovely, yes." Strong and handsome and humorous, and clearly intelligent. "But he is not like . . ."

"Like Isaac?" Hannah sighed. "I sometimes think Isaac is going to change the world and be remembered forever. But he is not like other men, and he will hurt you without even realising it."

"I thank you, Hannah, for your concern. But I would like to see him before I attend to my errands."

"I merely suggest that you take care, Sarah. The heart is a strange organ. It can lead us astray. Think on what I've said."

"I will."

"You'll find Isaac around somewhere. I heard him only ten minutes ago, muttering to himself as he wandered past.

She whirled round. Isaac was striding towards her, holding some papers

And do call back here before you leave. I shall give you some cakes to take home."

"Thank you." Sarah managed a smile. She knew that Hannah was only saying what everyone was saying, but it did not make it any easier to hear. She heard similar from her mother often enough.

****

She walked to the front of the house. Mary and Freddie were in the field, haring around, laughing breathlessly. Mary tripped and went down.

"Mary!" Sarah darted forward.

But her sister was up in a flash and off once again, still laughing. No harm done, apart from a dirty and possibly torn dress.

"Ah, there you are, Miss Sarah!"

She whirled round. Isaac was striding towards her, holding some papers.

"How fine to see you this morning. I wanted to discuss some points with you."

Isaac's hair was wild, his shirt untidy. Too concerned, he was, with thinking to be bothered about how he looked.

He was twenty-four and the most brilliant man she had ever known. Her heart skipped at the mere sight of him.

"Points?" she said.

"About your theories."

Sarah now recognised the papers as her own, the ones she had left with Isaac last time she visited. She could also see the papers were no longer neat. They were filled with extra writing. Well, untidy scrawls, really. Figures and equations. Diagrams. Crammed into every space.

"Your musings on the science of attraction are most interesting." Isaac perched on the low wall and patted the spot next to him. "Foolish, yes. Sometimes downright stupid. But interesting nonetheless."

Sarah sat, marvelling at the excitement overflowing from this man. Excitement because of her, because of what she had given to him. If only he would see her as a woman too, as well as a fellow scientific investigator.

Criticism, she could take. Being treated as a foolish student was also acceptable. What Sarah found harder was that Isaac seemed not to notice her femininity, not matter what effort she put in to making herself presentable.

"You make an assertion here –" Isaac stabbed a finger at the papers he had filled with his own calculations " – but you do not follow it through.

"The statement is ill-thought-out. In amongst the nonsense is the seed of a great notion. However, it needs more work. It needs developing.

"Had you seen what this assumption implied, then you could have easily . . ."

Sarah knew her own musings were nothing compared to the wonders that Isaac's brain could compose. She knew a great deal about many things. Yet she was a dullard compared to the great Isaac Newton.

She was almost entirely self-taught. Her father, a teacher, had an extensive library of science books and her innate curiosity about the world around her had led her to read and re-read them.

She questioned her father endlessly, but it was not long before she was asking questions which neither he nor his books could answer.

Then Isaac had returned home because of that awful plague last year which closed Cambridge University. She had passed Woolsthorpe Manor by chance and met him.

She was dazzled by his brilliance. Smitten. Madly in love within weeks.

And with no one else even close to her own level of expertise, she tentatively asked him to look over some ideas she had concerning the properties of light. He laughed when he saw them – not › out of contempt for petty ramblings, but because, he said, her ideas so closely matched his own.

"Are you reading my mind, dear girl?"

He had gazed at her in a way no man had done before. As an equal.

Well, not an equal. That was laughable. No one was Isaac's equal. Yet he did not look at her as if she were wasting his time. Her opinion mattered.

Sarah's mother, of course, hated her scientific investigations. They were not seemly. Her father, knowing his place in the family, publicly agreed with his wife. In private, he was more encouraging.

Yet even he expressed a worry that Sarah was creating a life for herself that was unsustainable. Women simply could not achieve what she was attempting to.

current thinking – and highly illuminating."

Sarah was concentrating on Isaac's words, but she had also seen the sparkle in his eyes and heard the excitement in his voice. His fingers had drawn frantic diagrams in the air and she imagined those fingers touching her cheek.

She wanted to lean in and kiss him. Oh, how wanton! Would he be shocked? Pleased? Indifferent?

He stood up abruptly.

"I need to ponder on this further. I have the glimmerings of an answer to the whole question of attraction between bodies, but it strangely eludes me at this present moment."

"I have further notes." Sarah held forward the papers she had brought with her. "Just some clarifications."

He gazed at Sarah, his eyes wide. "You are, my dear girl, amazing!"

Science was men's business. Women's bubbling thoughts and flighty natures were simply not suited to such serious matters.

However Sarah was convinced she knew better. She was convinced that one day she and Isaac would stand side by side, as husband and wife, as equals.

". . . while not entirely satisfactory, these idea of yours," Isaac was saying, "concerning the science of attraction between isolated bodies are most intriguing indeed. Your example regarding the orbit of the moon. I had never thought of the subject in this precise way before."

He looked up and stared at the moon still hanging in the daytime sky.

"You wonderful thing!" he exclaimed.

"I beg your . . ." Sarah realised with a start and a heavy heart that he was talking about the moon, and not her.

"Your theory is dramatically different to

Isaac took the papers from her and studied them, flipping from sheet to sheet, muttering to himself.

"Amazing!" He gazed at Sarah, his eyes wide, his smile tremendous. "You are, my dear girl, amazing!"

Her heart almost burst.

"I shall need space now and silence to work out the implications of what you are suggesting. So I shall say good day to you." He bowed politely and stalked away.

Sarah's heart almost burst again, but differently this time.

So that was that. Her ideas were amazing. But she, clearly, was not.

She could see it now. Isaac loved her ideas. He might even love her brain. But Isaac did not see her like that.

He was not nervously shy with her, afraid to let his true feelings show. He did not try to accidentally brush his hand against hers. He was the most wonderful ›

man she could ever imagine existing, but he hardly saw her at all.

He thought only of science.

How right they had all been.

"Miss Sarah! Miss Sarah!" Freddie had appeared. "You seen your Mary?"

"Mary? No. Why?"

"We'm playing, Miss Sarah. 'Ide and go find. Only Mary's run off and I can't find 'er nowhere. And it ain't fun no more. But if you . . ." Freddie paused. "'Ere, what's Mr Newton up to now?"

Sarah looked towards Isaac. He had stopped and was pointing at the moon, which had descended closer to the horizon. His pointing finger then tracked across the sky and back again. He shook his head and stared at the ground.

"He's thinking, Freddie." Sarah ruffled the boy's hair. "You should try it sometimes."

"Geroff!" Freddie laughed and ran off, calling out, "Mary!"

****

Sarah looked back at Isaac. She decided it was time. Now or never. Isaac might not see her as a woman. But he could be made to. She strode after him.

"Isaac. One moment. I need to speak with you. Isaac?"

Isaac continued to wander away.

"Isaac!" she called more sharply.

He did not respond. He was lost in a world only he could see, his racing mind oblivious to the sound of her voice.

So that was it. Sarah knew she could not keep waiting for him. Could not keep chasing him. Because it would forever be just like this.

It was then that she saw her sister.

Mary was in the apple tree, high up among the branches and the leaves. Sarah couldn't even begin to wonder what her sister's dress must be like after climbing up there. Mary saw she had been spotted and put her hand to her mouth to cover her mischievous giggle.

Sarah drew breath to call to her, but Mary held a finger to her lips.

Sarah swallowed back her call and watched as Isaac chose that tree to go and sit under. He began reading Sarah's papers again, muttering and tracing his finger across her work.

Mary looked down, giggling again. She could be so naughty.

Sarah almost called out to warn Isaac, but it was too late.

Mary plucked an apple, took aim and carefully let it drop.

The apple hit Isaac Newton, a glancing blow off his forehead, then rolled away across the grass.

Isaac looked stunned for a few moments, but never once did he look up. He stared instead into the middle distance. Sarah could almost hear his brain working. He reached for the apple, then tossed it upwards a few inches, catching it, repeating the action again and again, as if testing a hypothesis.

Abruptly, he stood.

"I have it!" He laughed. "I have it!"

Suddenly he was running. Running towards Sarah.

Sarah gasped. She smiled expectantly, and hopefully.

"It's gravity!" he shouted as he approached.

But then he ran straight past her, as though she were not even there, and disappeared into the house.

And Sarah realised Isaac might have suddenly understood – with a little help from herself and Mary – something profound about gravity's attraction, but he would never be able to comprehend human attraction.

Although, after all, who does?

By Steve Beresford

RECIPES AND FOOD STYLING: KATHRYN HAWKINS PHOTOGRAPHY: STUART MACGREGOR

Brunch Toast Tarts

Ingredients (Makes 8)

- **40g soft dairy or plant butter**
- **8 slices of bread from a 400g loaf, crusts removed**
- **8 thin rashers streaky bacon, halved**
- **50g button mushrooms, sliced**
- **12 cherry tomatoes, halved**
- **Salt and freshly ground black pepper**
- **4 medium eggs, beaten**

1 Preheat the oven to 200°C, Fan 180°C, Gas Mark 6. Use some of the butter to grease 8 muffin tins.

2 Roll bread slices thinly using a rolling pin. Spread with butter and cut in half. Push 2 pieces, butter-side up, into each muffin tin to make a case. Bake for 10 minutes.

3 Line each case with 2 pieces of bacon and add mushrooms and cherry tomatoes. Season the beaten eggs and pour into each case. Bake for about 20 minutes until cooked through.

4 Serve warm in paper cases, sprinkled with chopped parsley.

A Pergola Predicament

For Beth, her garden was the expression of her free, joyous spirit. For her neighbour, it was something very different

Beth hummed softly while balancing on the ladder, hammer in hand, enjoying the warm morning sun casting a golden glow over her garden.

She felt a thrill of satisfaction as she banged a hook into the pergola's wooden strut, preparing to hang the small bamboo wind chime she'd bought when backpacking in Thailand.

Those days were behind her now and, since moving into the maisonette six months ago, transforming this small outside space was her dream. With her dad's help, that dream was unfolding.

"Beth."

A stern voice interrupted her thoughts.

Looking down, she saw her neighbour, James, standing at the fence. She smiled.

"Hi, James. Did you have a nice holiday in Mexico?"

In his mid-thirties, dressed in drab, brown cords, grey T-shirt and navy cardigan, he looked older than his years.

The only thing they had in common was their age. She loved colourful outfits and, believing herself to be a free spirit, would never have chosen an archaeological guided tour like the one James had just returned from. Beth preferred to discover places under her own steam, at her own pace.

"Yes, thanks, the trip was good, but what's going on here?" he asked.

"A pergola. Dad helped me put it up."

"While I was away and against my fence! You do realise there are building regulations for outside structures? Any chance you can come down please, so we can discuss this?"

"OK, but I'm sure my dad checked the regulations." Beth shrugged.

"Can I remind you that I'm an architect, Beth, and know about such things? There are covenants on this estate you might not be aware of."

Had Beth possessed hackles, they'd have risen. James sounded so pompous.

"Fine, but first I'll finish putting up my wind chime," she said.

"You do realise there are building regulations for outside structures?"

James's eyes widened in horror.

"One of those clanking things?"

Beth grimaced.

"It's bamboo. The sound is soothing."

"Not everyone thinks so, Beth," he said with a sigh. "Look, why not pop over to mine so we discuss this civilly over a cup of tea?"

Beth had had a few brief conversations ›

IMAGES: DCT

with James since she'd moved in, mostly about the weather, a quick chat about her job in HR and he'd let her know he'd be away on holiday, yet she hadn't been inside his house. One neighbour a few doors down, Mrs Thompson, had mentioned that his wife had passed away three years ago, and how he'd become rather introverted since. This made his invitation seem even more daunting.

She stepped down from the ladder and glanced around her garden. Wildflowers mingled freely with herbs and an old wooden crate served as a planter for trailing vines. A carved stone birdbath she'd picked up at a salvage yard stood in the middle of the tufty lawn. She planned to create a beautiful garden structure with the pergola, hang bottles containing citronella candles and wrap fairy lights around the struts.

With a mixture of frustration and determination bubbling inside her, she headed for next door.

****

Beth perched on a high stool at the breakfast bar while James made tea. She gazed around at the immaculate kitchen, a sleek modern design, with gleaming stainless-steel appliances on black granite and handle-less glossy grey cabinets. It was such a contrast to her own mismatched vintage cupboards painted in cheerful pastels and wooden countertops crowded with jars of spices, potted herbs and well-loved cookbooks.

James placed a white cup and saucer in front of her and sat opposite.

"Thanks," she said, taking a sip of the tea. She glanced out of the window at his garden that mirrored the precision of his kitchen, with meticulously pruned shrubs and an abstract marble sculpture in the middle of a manicured lawn.

"Your garden is very . . . neat and tidy."

"Exactly how I like it. As you can see, the pergola is quite intrusive, towering over my fence."

"I wouldn't say towering," she ventured, although she had to admit it was more visible than she imagined from his side. In fact, if she were honest, she hadn't considered what it would look like from his garden, only thought it best to erect it while he was on holiday so the noise wouldn't disturb him.

The fine lines that fanned out were evidence that he'd once laughed

She stole a glance at his face. His eyes were as blue as the cornflowers she grew and the fine lines that fanned out from the corners were evidence that he'd once laughed, although she'd only ever seen him give a quick smile.

"I really don't know what you expect me to do, James." She picked up her cup and drained her tea. Although she preferred it strong, she was glad too much milk had cooled the tea enough for her to finish it quickly.

His face assumed a steely expression.

"I'd expect you to lower it, but preferably take the whole lot down."

"That's not going to happen," she said calmly, determined not to let him see she was shaken by the suggestion. She stood up. "I think I'd better go."

"OK, but this isn't over, Beth."

As soon as she got back, she called her dad to fill him in on the dispute. He suggested that as a gesture, she remove the wind chime.

Beth blew out her cheeks. So much for bamboo dispersing negative energy and attracting positive vibes!

Her dad confirmed he'd checked online for building regulations before she bought the structure.

"I didn't find anything that flagged up a problem. Do you remember your solicitor mentioning anything about estate covenants when you bought the flat?"

Beth hadn't, but would have to dig out the paperwork and double-check. Her eyes filled with tears and momentarily she wished she'd never bought the place.

Then she reminded herself it was close to work and friends, and she'd adored putting her own stamp on the interior and doing the same outside.

"Thanks, Dad. I appreciate your help."

"Any time, love. I'm sure everything will be just fine."

Over the next few days, she and James merely gave a polite nod if they saw each other. Then, arriving home from work one evening, she stepped into her hallway and dropped her keys in the bowl. Her eyes fell on a brown envelope lying on the doormat. She tore it open and as she read the contents, her chest squeezed.

Dear Ms Turner

This is to inform you we have received a complaint regarding the construction of a pergola on your property. It has come to our attention this structure may not comply with local building regulations. As a result, a planning officer from the council will visit you on the 21st at 2pm to carry out an inspection.

Yours sincerely

The Residents' Association

****

Three days later, Beth, having taken an afternoon off work, paced nervously in her kitchen. When the doorbell rang, she rushed to answer it.

A tall man stood on the doorstep.

"Mr Gupta, planning officer," he said, showing her a photo ID.

"Come in," she said, stepping aside. With a polite smile but thumping heart, she led him through to the garden and watched as he checked the pergola's height and distance from the boundary with his laser measure.

After what seemed like an endless lot of measuring and recording in a notebook, Mr Gupta turned to Beth.

"Everything seems to be within the permitted development guidelines," he said. "I'll email a copy of my findings to you and the complainant. I must say, your pergola looks very nice. You've done a good job."

Relief flooded through Beth.

"Thank you so much."

As soon as Mr Gupta left, Beth pulled out her phone, dialled her dad's number and let him know the good news.

And yet, she couldn't shake off a lingering sense of unease. What would James's reaction be when he received the report? As much as she had "won", she didn't want to upset James even more.

****

After a restless night, she woke with an idea. Once showered and dressed, she grabbed her car keys and headed out.

At the garden centre, she loaded the last of the climbers into her car and hoped the splurge on her credit card would be worthwhile. Her plan was for the plants to transform the pergola, soften its edges and bring colour and fragrance, all of which would benefit James as well as her. As she went to shut the boot, she spotted her neighbour, Mrs Thompson, carrying a new watering can.

"Hello, Beth," Mrs Thompson said, walking across to Beth's car. "I see you've splashed out there." ›

"That's right. Climbers for my pergola to improve how it looks," she replied, glancing at the array of plants.

Mrs Thompson nodded, but frowned.

"I heard about the pergola problem on the grapevine, excuse the pun." She gave a wry smile. "I know you mean well with these plants but . . ." She hesitated. "James isn't a fan of flowers. He got rid of all his after his wife passed away."

"Oh, no! Do you know why?"

Mrs Thompson shook her head.

"We saw the skip arrive and him filling it up, but none of us wanted to interfere."

"Well," Beth said, brightly. "Perhaps he didn't want the upkeep. Hopefully he'll benefit from these without having to look after them."

"Of course, dear. I'm sure the plants will look beautiful, but keep in mind that James might not think so."

Beth carried the pots through to her garden, her buoyant mood diminishing as she replayed in her mind the conversation with Mrs Thompson.

With a heavy sigh, she positioned the pots where she would plant them. The honeysuckle was the most well established, already in flower, smelling strong and sweet. The jasmine was almost as large, with a musky scent, and the colours of the passionflowers, vibrant.

So James might not approve, but what option did she have but to carry out her vision for the pergola?

****

The following day, Beth planted the climbers, adding mulch and water. Swiping the back of her hand across her damp brow, she surveyed her work. The leaves shimmered in the sunlight and the blossoms wafted in the gentle breeze. She saw James peering over the fence.

"I had the email from Planning," he said, looking downcast. "Seems I don't have a leg to stand on."

Beth had received the message too. On a night out, when she'd relayed the events to her friend Amy, the young woman had dismissed them.

"Don't waste any more time worrying about James's feelings. You're in the right and he'll just have to suck it up."

But Beth felt sad about the situation. Maybe because she worked in HR and dealt with a lot of problems, she had a predisposition to solve them.

"I can see and smell that you're going to make the thing even more obvious with all those plants," James said. I hope you'll keep them under control."

"Just make sure they don't come over the fence," came the curt reply

Beth felt her cheeks grow warm, but she smiled and said, "I think they'll make the pergola softer and we'll both be able to enjoy the colour and fragrance."

"Just make sure they don't come over the fence," came the curt reply.

Beth nodded.

"I understand. I'll make sure I keep them trimmed."

He gave a nod and walked away, leaving Beth with a mix of frustration and sadness. She bent her face to the honeysuckle bloom, inhaling the delicious scent. She'd read somewhere it was possible to make jam from the flowers. Not that she wanted to pick them, but she had an inkling of what to do next.

****

It was almost midday on Sunday when ›

Beth arranged the newly baked scones on a plate with a generous dollop of strawberry jam. Taking a deep breath, she walked over to James's front door and knocked. She'd been up early, but had waited until now to deliver them in case he enjoyed a long lie on a Sunday.

After a moment, James opened the door, surprise flickering across his face.

Beth cleared her throat.

"Hi. I made scones earlier and wondered if you'd like a few. If I'm honest, they're actually a peace offering. I really didn't think the pergola would cause you any problem."

With a heavy sigh, James took the plate. "Thanks. That's very thoughtful of you." He was silent for a moment, looking down at the scones. When he spoke, his voice cracked.

"I remember, after my wife's funeral, Mrs Thompson brought me a casserole and a shepherd's pie." He met Beth's eyes and gave a little smile. "Food can be such a comfort, can't it?"

Beth saw the tension in his face ease a little, revealing warmth and depth in his eyes. He opened the door wide.

"Would you like to come in?"

Beth nodded, feeling a sense of hope.

"I'd like that very much."

An hour previously, Beth would never have thought she'd be sitting with James on his patio, enjoying a coffee and scones. She glanced at the pergola, imagining how much nicer it would look covered in the plants, and then the neat row of shrubs at the end of the garden.

"I can see you like greenery."

James nodded. "Easier to manage than fussing over flowers."

She took a sip of coffee.

"I suppose it is for some people. Although after my mum died, my dad said that tending to the rose bushes they both loved made him feel close to her."

James turned to look at her kindly.

"I'm sorry to hear you lost your mum," he said gently.

Beth nodded.

"It was over ten years ago, but I still miss her. Luckily, my dad is fit and well."

There was a pause, with James staring into the distance. Then he spoke.

"Emily loved plants, especially ones with a powerful scent. Climbing roses on the fence, jasmine on a trellis and so on. After she passed away, I couldn't bear the reminder. I ripped them out in a frenzy.

"She cared for them, you see, more than she did for herself. She ignored her symptoms, yet at the first sign of disease in her plants she searched for solutions."

"Oh, how tragic," Beth murmured. "I'd never have bought all those plants if I'd known they'd trigger painful memories."

James shook his head. "Please don't think that. It's time I started facing up to the memories, not running from them." He looked down at his hands. "Actually, Emily had a book about climbing plants. Maybe you'd like to borrow it?"

"It would be an honour."

They sat in silence for a moment. As Beth closed her eyes, she took a deep breath and was taken aback by a strong floral aroma enveloping her, as if the entire garden was in full bloom. It must be her imagination – her newly planted climbers couldn't possibly be that intense.

James broke the silence.

"I'm thinking that maybe I could plant something colourful in the garden as a tribute to my wife."

"What a lovely idea," Beth said softly. "I know for a fact there's a pastel pink fragrant rose called Emily. Dad has one."

"Sounds perfect," James said.

Beth smiled. At last, healing and, hopefully, a new friendship could bloom

By Claire Buckle

Brain Boosters

Sudoku

			2		1			
	5						6	
			5		4			
			3		9			
3			8		6			1
	9	6				8	4	
1								7
9		8				6		2
5		4	1		2	3		8

Fill in each of the blank squares with the numbers 1 to 9, so that each row, each column and each 3x3 cell contains all the numbers from 1 to 9.

Turn To Page 171 For Solutions

Word Wheel

You have ten minutes to find as many words as possible using the letters in the wheel. Each word must be three letters or more and contain the central letter. Use each letter once and no plurals, foreign words or proper nouns are allowed. There is at least one nine-letter word.

Forgive Me, Please

Visiting fills me with an unbearable sense of loss . . . but we should never give up on those we love

I took ages to choose this Mother's Day card, with its flowery writing, cheesy sentiments and line drawing of two shadowy figures walking hand-in-hand along a sunlit beach.

It feels awkward in my hot hands as I stand on the pavement, gazing at the entrance to Solent View Home for the Elderly. The building stands tall, white, familiar. Outwardly at least, nothing much alters here.

I take a deep breath and climb up the stone steps to the double doors. The gravel path is edged with bright daffodils and purple crocuses that promise new life, which sits poorly with a building I associate so strongly with loss.

It's only been four weeks of "Maybe-Saturdays" and "Hopefully-Sundays," but I can imagine Mum's changed so much since I last visited, it might as well have been four years.

Forgive me, please . . .

It's hard to accept that, little by little, I'm losing the woman who was once my heroine. Mum's still alive, but she's not here any more. It makes me feel sad, distant. I'm ashamed to say that – other than dropping in a bundle of photos and memorabilia last week, as requested by the nurse – I haven't visited Solent View for a month.

I find any excuse not to call in. Mum's creeping dementia has robbed her of her memory and turned me into a coward.

I ring the bell.

"Morning, Kate," says Nancy, the nursing assistant, who leads me to a small desk in reception.

"H . . . hello." I smile, tightly.

I feel guilty. She'll be all too aware how long it is since I last properly visited.

Mum's still alive, but she's not here any more. It makes me feel sad, distant

Forgive me, please . . .

But I'm here now, I want to counter. *Surely that counts.*

I sign the register, trying to ignore the smells of soup and ammonia and the lack of energy in the stifling air.

"How's Mum . . . been?" I ask.

She passes me a lanyard and smiles as I slip it over my head.

"Well, I think you'll notice a change. We've been trying something new."

What could that be? Another drug perhaps, or a different therapy?

Once upon a time her words would have filled me with hope to match the new season, but not now. This is a place ›

IMAGES: DCT

I've journeyed to before. The doctors have tried diet changes, various drugs, an exercise plan – but nothing really works.

I follow her down the corridor and we pass through the communal lounge.

"Morning," I smile, nodding at the other residents – the "good" ones – who sit in the large hot room, like greenhouse tomatoes, facing away from the television which is always on but never watched.

But Mum's not sitting with them; she's upstairs now.

It was this move from downstairs to upstairs that had scared me the most and stopped me visiting.

****

When I last visited Mum in the home, it had been February. Cold, damp, grey. Declan, the male nurse – plump, dark-haired, smiley – had led me to Mum's new room, along dark corridors, trying hard to put a positive spin on the momentous shift of location.

We all feared "upstairs". It was where the most poorly residents moved to.

When I'd asked him how Mum had been, he'd answered, "Noisy."

That one stark word had told me everything and nothing.

"Help me, Mum . . . Mum," she'd wailed, a dry-mouthed call that had chilled my bones and snapped my heart.

In her head, she was a little girl who couldn't understand where her mother had gone and why she wouldn't come, no matter how many times she called for her.

What could I say to her? What on earth could I do to help?

Ignoring her cries, I'd touched her hand and as Declan left us alone, I'd greeted her with my usual excuse.

"Hello, Mum. Sorry I've not stopped by. I've been busy. You know how it is."

Forgive me, please . . .

She'd been lying all twisted, so I'd called for Declan. He'd returned with another male nurse who'd bustled in with a too-wide smile and an empty frown.

"Come on, Molly," he'd said.

With strong arms, he'd moved Mum so that she wasn't slumped.

"Thank you," I'd said, while inside I raged, angry that no one here called her by the right name.

It's not Molly and it's not Mrs Lane. It's Milly. Why are you so careless? I'd wanted to scream.

But my anger was misplaced. It was me I was cross with.

"Has anyone tried a Life Story book?" he asked when I'd kissed Mum goodbye

Declan had pushed open the door to room four and I'd gasped. I'd expected Mum to look less well and less robust, but the sight of her in her new room that day had shocked me.

Upstairs, she'd been a breathing skeleton, lying in a padded cot, drifting between the here-and-now and the ever-after, with her too-thin face and open mouth that called out for her own mother who'd gone to her grave twenty years ago.

For never being here, and for looking to strangers to care while I frantically made out that I was busy elsewhere.

Forgive me, please . . .

I'd reached out and touched Mum's curly white hair. It needed a wash, but who at the home really cared about her appearance?

The walls had pushed in on me in the tiny room with its four-foot-square window, beyond which the living world outside had teased, *Remember me?*

I'd glanced around. Would I eventually lie in a bed like this? Window-shopping for a life that had once been?

On a shelf by the door were three photos of the Mum I used to know.

One was taken of her behind the bar of the Rose and Crown pub where she'd been the landlady.

Another was of her wedding day; she'd looked like a glamorous film star.

The last one was of me, aged about three, looking over the top of my teddy's head with the cheekiest smile on my face.

"Do you remember . . ." I'd asked, but my words had died on my lips.

Mum struggled to recognise me; she'd certainly have forgotten these pictures.

Was this all life amounted to in the end? A shelf with three photos, a nurse calling you by the wrong name and a daughter who promised, "I really will come and see you again soon. Maybe-Saturday or Hopefully-Sunday."

Forgive me, please . . .

****

It had been the photos on the shelf that had given Declan the idea.

"Has anyone tried a Life Story book?" he asked when I'd kissed Mum goodbye after that ridiculously short visit four Sundays ago.

"Life story?" I'd frowned.

"Yes – we've started using them for a few clients."

Declan explained that they'd filled folders with photos, text and mementoes to use as memory aids.

"If it's done properly, it can be a real benefit. Not only to the client, but to family and staff. Would you be interested?"

It sounded a good idea, but we'd already tried so many things and Mum was deteriorating.

"Drop in a few photos, some keepsakes. Jot down a few of Molly's . . ."

"Milly's."

"Sorry – Milly's milestones and we can create a book especially for her."

I'd nodded and, later in the week, I'd pulled out a few photos, a dozen of the old coins she used to collect, some old recipes I'd found in a drawer and several other bits and pieces I thought Solent View could use. After I'd left the bag in reception, I'd forgotten about it.

That experience in room four on the previous Sunday afternoon had haunted me, pushing me firmly away. I'd have stayed away, I think, if visiting this Sunday hadn't been unavoidable. It was Mother's Day, after all . . .

****

Nurse Nancy is ahead of me and I think she's going the wrong way. She's not climbing the stairs to room four; she's striding off down the corridor towards the conservatory.

"Nancy?"

I feel a bit miffed – can't they get anything right here?

She turns.

"You OK, Kate?"

"Mum – she's in room four now."

She smiles.

"She was, yes. Milly's in the conservatory today."

I'm puzzled. I thought once clients went upstairs, they stayed upstairs. Maybe it's something to do with Mothering Sunday.

The conservatory is bright, with rows of rattan armchairs. Sunlight slices through the long windows which overlook the perfectly mown lawn.

They have gorgeous grounds here at Solent View. It must be the sea air. Thriving in busy borders are a host of red tulips, marigolds, the blush of pink › magnolia and knots of polyanthus.

At first I can't see her, but then I spot Mum at the end of the conservatory. Her white hair's been washed and she's gazing at her lap. Despite the warmth, there's a tartan blanket wrapped around her straw-thin legs.

If nothing else, it's good to see her sitting in an armchair again.

I take a breath. This is always hard. The moment she looks up but doesn't see me. I grip the card as if it can give me strength. I nod and smile at the other residents. Some have visitors; some of them are alone.

"Happy Mother's Day, Mum." I smile, not expecting a response.

But this time, she reacts. This time, she points and mumbles, "Ted."

I'm happy. Mum hasn't spoken directly to me in a while and although I'm angered when *she's* addressed by the wrong name, I don't mind that she hasn't called me Kate.

Nancy tucks the blanket around her legs and says, "Kate's here to see you."

As I sit beside her, I can see there's an open folder on her lap. And suddenly I understand. I *am* Ted!

"That's me, Mum. With my old teddy."

It's the photo from her shelf, of me holding the teddy bear. It's no longer in her room; it's in this folder.

"It's early days, Kate." Nancy smiles. "But Milly's enjoying the Life Story book."

"Can I look through it?" I ask Mum.

She just stares, so I take it gently from her bony hands. Flicking through the pages, it's like taking a magical mystery tour of our past.

"Look – our old house." I remember not to bombard her with too many words as I stare at a coloured shot of our semi in Mayfield Road.

Over the page are stuck some of the coins she used to collect. Mum's finger traces the outline of an old penny. Slowly, I start to talk to her about the contents in the folder; all I can remember.

Time slips away from us and I'm surprised when Nancy says, gently,

"It's time for Milly's tea now, Kate."

Normally I'm long gone before suppertime, but having the folder has given shape to my visit.

"I'd better be off now. Oh, I almost forgot. Here," I smile, handing Mum the card. I help her open the envelope. "For you – it's Mother's Day. Thank you for everything you ever did."

Tears prick my eyes as I hug her.

Flicking through the pages, it's like taking a magical mystery tour

"Shall I stick the card in the folder? Add to her Life Story?" Nancy asks.

When I frown, she smiles.

"Your mum's story hasn't ended. It's still evolving."

I like that, I think, as I prepare to leave Solent View.

"Will you come next Sunday, Kate?"

I look at Nancy. "Yes, I think I will."

"It helps, doesn't it? The folder."

I nod. "It does. Thank you."

Walking down the stone steps, I think how this is the first visit in a long time I've enjoyed. The Life Story book has helped me as much as it has Mum.

As I make my way to my car, I don't mentally ask, *Forgive me, please . . .*

I think that, perhaps, I'm finally learning to forgive myself.

By Tess Niland Kimber

Brain Boosters

Codeword

Each letter of the alphabet has been replaced by a number. The numbers for the first name of a celebrity are given. Work out which number represents which letter to reveal the stage musical that Alfie Boe is best known for.

16	18	11	25	16	9		16	22	18	25	4	5	20	
4		25		25		16		18		6		2		3
2	16	9	11	7	5	14	16	25		25	26	11	2	4
12		11		24		4		16		1		10		7
12	25	7	5	2	5	13		9	2	12	12	14	26	10
23		5		11		15				9				10
	16	9	18	26		2	7	9	20		9	15	25	25
15		25		25		11		18		7		2		19
7	14	19	25		7	1	25	26		1	14	1	25	
4				16				10		24		7		8
9	20	7 A	26	13	25	19		16	9	11	7	26	10	25
17		4 L		14		11		9		2		20		9
25	4	3 F	14	26		2	21	25	11	16	20	2	2	9
19		14 I		26		4		26		14		2		25
	11	25 E	5	23	5	4	25		5	7	26	19	14	19

A B C D E F G H I J K L M N O P Q R S T U V W X Y Z

1	2	3 F	4 L	5	6	7 A	8	9	10	11	12	13
14 I	15	16	17	18	19	20	21	22	23	24	25 E	26

4 L	25 E	16	1	14 I	16	25 E	11	7 A	24	4 L	25 E	16

Turn To Page 171 For Solutions

Beetroot and Apple Soup

Ingredients (Serves 4)

- **1tbsp sunflower oil**
- **2 red onions, chopped**
- **700g beetroot, peeled and cubed**
- **250g Bramley apple, peeled and cubed**
- **1 litre vegetable stock**
- **Salt and freshly ground black pepper**
- **75g soft goat's cheese**
- **75g Greek yogurt**
- **40g hot horseradish sauce**
- **1 garlic clove, finely chopped**
- **Few sprigs tarragon, chopped**
- **2tbsp chopped walnuts**

1 Heat the oil in saucepan, add the onions and sauté for 6-7 minutes to soften. Stir in the beetroot, apple and the stock. Season with salt and freshly ground black pepper. Bring to the boil, cover and simmer for 30 minutes, or until the beetroot is tender.

2 Meanwhile in a small bowl mix together the goat's cheese, yogurt, horseradish sauce and garlic. Set aside. Transfer the soup to a food processor, in batches if necessary, and whiz to a purée.

3 Return the soup to the cleaned saucepan and reheat. Adjust the seasoning, if necessary and divide between four warmed soup bowls. Place spoonfuls of the cheese mix in the centre and sprinkle over a little tarragon and chopped walnuts. Serve immediately.

RECIPES AND FOOD STYLING: JENNIE SHAPTER
FOOD PHOTOGRAPHY: JON WHITAKER

Rye bread makes a delicious accompaniment for this soup

The Easter Bonnie

Can a chocoholic's friendship with a health fanatic survive the annual village chocolate frenzy?

Bonnie's tongue stuck out in concentration as she squeezed the piping bag with all the energy her aching forearms could muster.

Pink icing shot out of the nozzle and hit the chocolate egg with a splat.

Bonnie picked up a toothpick and expertly transformed the pink blob into a cute little bunny face. She smiled, knowing the sugar-crazed kids of the village would be fighting over this tiny chocolate egg, with the lump of icing clinging to the side.

Kids love icing. Especially Bonnie Bonbon's famous white chocolate icing.

Hands on hips, Bonnie beamed around at her tiny chocolate shop. The chalkboard sign on the door was flipped to Closed, so there were no customers, but the room was full to its wonky wooden rafters.

Tray after tray of tiny, pastel-patterned chocolate eggs balanced precariously on every available surface. Bonnie knew every quirky nook and cranny of her little chocolaterie, so she was well aware which oak floorboards to avoid stepping on, lest she topple a tray on the other side of the room.

"*Magnifique*," she breathed to herself, inspecting the rows of iced pastel patterns, custard-yellow ducklings and powder-pink bunnies lovingly crafted onto each delicate ovoid of silky-smooth chocolate. Each of them was no bigger than a hen's egg.

The tiny room was heady with the scent of sugar and cocoa, and if Bonnie closed her eyes she could very well be standing in her childhood school hall, back in France . . .

****

Her tummy fluttered as the bell rang signalling the start of the Easter egg hunt – the *Chasse aux Oeufs.*

She could hear her classmates squealing with delight as they scattered around the schoolyard, hunting for the colourful eggs they'd spent that entire week enthusiastically decorating.

All was harmonious as bruised and satiated children scoffed their bounty

Touching a spot on her elbow that had never quite been the same since the Easter of '97, she could also remember the overenthusiastic "nudges" out of the way which occurred when the hunters caught sight of their prize.

Yet all was harmonious again as bruised and satiated children scoffed their bounty together at the end of the day. ›

PICTURES: DCT

As a chocoholic from an early age, Easter had always been Bonnie's most favourite time of year.

And now as a resident of this quaint British village, and proud, lifelong chocolate enthusiast, Bonnie had brought this treasured tradition over from France.

Every year for the past decade, Bonnie's Bonbons chocolate shop had partnered with various businesses in the local community to run a highly anticipated Easter Egg hunt for the local children. The only entry requirement was that each participant had to sport a homemade Easter bonnet.

As much as she loved chocolate, this was Bonnie's favourite part: the parade of paper crowns covered in pompoms, pipe cleaners and so much glitter that she had to clean up the school playground with a vacuum cleaner afterwards!

Bonnie couldn't stop smiling as she dropped the antique shutters, hiding the legion of eggs from view, and locked the door. Then she gave it an extra tug, in case the knot in the doorframe had swelled again thanks to the wonderful British weather.

The weather was not an aspect of British life Bonnie enjoyed; she frowned as she pulled the hood of her raincoat over her curly, hazel mane. Her patent boots clacked against the stones as she made the short trip to The Cobbles Café.

While many Brits might be found in the pub on a Saturday evening, you would always find Bonnie in the café. She was a creature of habit, and always hungry.

While she was a skilled chocolatier, Bonnie's skills for creating balanced, nourishing food were somewhat lacking.

The bell over the door tinkled as Bonnie waved to The Cobbles owner, chef, and village heart-throb, Harvey.

He nodded to her usual table which he kept reserved for her, in a cosy little booth by a window.

Bonnie's raincoat dripped across the stone floor, and she could see Harvey shaking his head as he brought over her usual order without her having to ask.

While some might apologise, Bonnie shrugged cheekily. She never felt awkward with Harvey.

Over the years of him providing her three meals a day, they'd built up a solid routine, and then a friendship.

As she tucked into her Spanish omelette she was grateful for her gifted friend

He'd been her first and best friend in England. Bonnie sometimes even wondered if there might be more between them, often catching herself admiring his strong shoulders and square, rugged jawline that held up a kind smile.

But then he would lecture her about her sugar intake, or her need to eat more vegetables, or inform her about the latest research into macronutrients.

A Sunday morning 5k run would be Harvey's dream date – and a waking nightmare for Bonnie. They were simply too different. But as she tucked into her Spanish omelette, she was grateful for her gifted friend.

Harvey heaved his giant frame into the wooden chair opposite her, relaxed his exhausted shoulders, and the pair caught each other up on their day.

Once she'd finished eating, Bonnie pushed her plate away, satisfied. She drained her hot chocolate and then declared, "Harvey, you've outdone yourself. That omelette was even better than usual, and the hot chocolate . . ." She mimed a chef's kiss.

"Well, my junk-food-fancying friend, the omelette was so good because I used a new high oleic oil and sourced some lovely baby spinach at the market. You need more iron in your diet."

Harvey smirked, proud that his latest efforts to improve Bonnie's nutritional intake had been well received.

Bonnie raised an eyebrow.

"And the hot chocolate? Please tell me there was no spinach in that."

Harvey laughed. "Nah, that was just an extra scoop of cocoa."

Bonnie raised her other eyebrow. Very out of character for Harvey the Healthy.

"What? I know you like it extra chocolatey, and I thought you deserved it after all the work you're doing for the Easter Egg hunt." Harvey looked sheepishly at the ground.

Bonnie dabbed her mouth with her napkin to hide her flushed cheeks.

"Right! We need to discuss the plan of attack for tomorrow, since this is the first year you're co-hosting."

The Cobbles Café was this year's co-sponsor of the Easter egg hunt, and Harvey had so far been the epitome of a silent partner.

This was fine with Bonnie: she had the whole affair down pat, and could run the Easter event bunny-hopping on one leg.

However Harvey was to be this year's bonnet adjudicator, and he needed to know the judging criteria.

Harvey groaned and slumped against his hand sulkily as Bonnie ran through the order of proceedings.

"What in the name of the Easter Bunny is wrong with you?" Bonnie demanded.

"I just hate Easter. Or, more, the over-commercialised glorification of gluttony." Harvey groaned.

Bonnie blinked, wondering whether this was gibberish, or if her English wasn't as good as she thought.

"What?"

Harvey rubbed at his face in frustration and explained.

"It's just an excuse for kids – and adults –" he looked pointedly at Bonnie – "to gorge on chocolate. To pig out and stuff their faces."

Bonnie began to protest, but Harvey held up a hand.

"Don't get me wrong, sweets are fine in moderation. But it's just so excessive. So indulgent. So greedy. So . . ."

"Fun?" Bonnie fumed, placing her money down on the table, then getting up to leave. She was fiercely defensive of her chocolate empire and the life it had given her, and was furious at her supposed co-host. Supposed friend.

Harvey sighed.

"Look, I don't mean to be an Easter humbug. I just don't think it's very healthy to be obsessed with chocolate. I just wish there was a bit more balance."

He gestured to the remains of Bonnie's supper on the table.

"I'll see you tomorrow in the schoolyard," Bonnie mumbled as she headed for the door, not meaning her farewell to sound as threatening as it did.

****

Bonnie downed a three-sugared caramel latte and rubbed her exhausted eyes. For once, it wasn't the influx of glucose that had kept her up late last night. She'd gone back and forth over what Harvey had said.

At first, she was furious that he'd turned this sweet tradition so bitter. Then she was fearful that she was unintentionally pushing these innocent children into a lifetime of unhealthy chocolate addiction.

It was 2am when the brainwave hit ›

her. There was no sleeping after that: just prep to be done, Pinterest projects to research and, of course, eggs to hide.

****

As the children skipped into the playground, Bonnie stood in front of a portable chalkboard she'd wheeled into the centre and shifted from foot to foot. She felt like that nervous little girl French girl on her first day at an English school all over again.

The kids were vibrating with excitement, squirming, flossing and hopping about. Their weary-looking parents tried to keep them in check, while clutching bags undoubtedly concealing their child's Easter Bonnet masterpieces.

"Can we start yet?" one particularly wriggly boy pleaded.

"Soon." Bonnie smiled sympathetically. "We just have to wait for Harvey – oh here he is!"

Harvey jogged through the crowd and mouthed, "Sorry" at Bonnie.

Bonnie saw the children dip into ready runners' stances, preparing for them to ring the bell and unleash the hunting party. Harvey picked up the bell, but she put her hand on his shoulder.

"Wait!"

The kids fell silent.

"We're doing things a bit differently this year," she began.

The crowd of pint-sized egg predators groaned. Bonnie raised her hands to quieten the mutineers.

"Don't worry, there'll still be eggs." A cheer. "But this year, you have to earn them." She flipped over the chalkboard to reveal a pastel masterpiece. A schedule of events was drawn up in chalk, outlining the happenings of the day.

"Miss Easter Bonnie," a little girl in glasses squeaked. "I can't read yet."

Bonnie melted like a chocolate fondant and saw Harvey do the same. So he did like kids.

"I know we all love chocolate, but it's not very healthy, is it?" Bonnie asked.

A begrudging "No" rumbled through the crowd.

"And we all know exercise is very healthy for us, isn't it? And it's fun!"

A firmer "Yes" echoed back.

"So we're going to have an Easter Sunday Funday! Lots of super-exciting races and games, and chocolate eggs for the winners!"

An excited cheer rang out, and a startled pigeon nearby made his getaway.

****

The pigeon was wise, as the entire village was soon roused by excited squeals and yells. Bonnie counted amost every curious business owner and village resident congregating in the schoolyard to investigate what was going on.

Many stayed to cheer on the children as they ran the "Re-lay an Egg" race, referee questionable hula-hooping techniques in the "Hula-Hop Until You Drop" marathon, and even joined in the "Easter Egg and Spoon" race.

When the hoarse crowd finally gathered around the chalkboard for the Easter Bonnet parade (traditions were traditions, after all) their faces were red, sweaty and plastered with smiles.

Bonnie beamed as she realised not only had she created a new healthier tradition that the children could enjoy every year, she'd reminded the older residents of more nostalgic days, when they would run around the playground and skin their knees or elbows.

She was so glad she could pay homage to her health-conscious friend, show her gratitude for all he had done for her since she'd moved to this sleepy village from across the Channel . . . ›

Wait. Where was Harvey? He was supposed to judge the Bonnet Parade!

After a fruitless scan of the crowd, Bonnie resigned herself to the idea that she would be hosting this event as well. She was annoyed that Harvey had bailed after all the effort she'd put in to including him and his values. But mainly, she was excited to judge the parade.

****

Refreshed by cups of water, a stream of adorable miniature fashion models strutted across the playground, swishing their tutu skirts and stomping their wellied feet. They proudly supported towering paper crowns, bowing under the weight of poster-painted rabbits, plastic gemstones and glitter-encrusted eggs. The crowd went wild for each of them.

Bonnie was now more irritated that Harvey had disappeared, leaving her to make such a tough decision alone.

The crowd was silent for the first time in hours as they gathered for the judge's verdict. Bonnie diplomatically bestowed the coveted prize on a little boy in overalls and purple wellies. He was so busy trying to stop his towering bonnet of bunnies and papier-mâché eggs from toppling, he didn't even realise he'd won!

As the village summoned up hoarse voices to cheer and clap the victor, Bonnie felt a tug on her raincoat. She looked down to see the girl in glasses who couldn't read, blinking up at her.

"Mrs Easter Bonnie, my legs weren't fast enough today. I didn't win any chocolate." Her voice trailed off as she tried to remain brave, and a single tear escaped down her pink cheeks.

Bonnie dropped to her knees, swallowing this sweet child in a hug.

"Don't worry, sweetie!" Harvey's deep voice rang out from behind her. "That's what the Egg Hunt is for!"

The crowd exploded in applause and the little girl beamed, as Bonnie turned to see her very serious friend Harvey – usually head to toe in ethical designer sportswear – in a bubblegum-pink, furry rabbit onesie. He'd scrawled lopsided whiskers on his cheeks, which were flushed from embarrassment.

But his smile was genuine as he clanged the bell and the children scattered around the schoolyard.

The pair laughed at a nearby gaggle of kids, noisily appreciating their first finds.

"I'm starving after all that running around!" one said between mouthfuls.

Harvey shrugged at Bonnie.

"It's all about balance. I certainly think you've earned one of these today." From a furry pocket, Harvey produced a pastel-painted egg and handed it to Bonnie.

Nudging his fluffy shoulder, she brought out a black and white painted egg – an Easter Humbug.

"And you've definitely earned this."

Harvey took the egg from her, his pink paw brushing Bonnie's fingers.

"Maybe we could have them for dessert? You could come back to the café, and I could make us something for dinner. Something special."

Bonnie looked at his wonky whiskers, that kind smile, and his broad shoulders bulging out of his ridiculous bunny suit. Within that onesie was a thoughtful man, who concerned himself daily with ensuring she lived healthily, ate something other than chocolate and takeaways, had listened to her every day for the past five years and did the most ridiculous things to make her happy.

She nodded eagerly, and took his paw as they walked back to The Cobbles.

It seemed inevitable really. The perfect pair: a gym bunny and an Easter bunny.

By Lauren Rebbeck

Chicken and Summer Veg Bake

Ingredients (Serves 2-3)

- **180g macaroni (or other pasta tubes)**
- **1 courgette, sliced**
- **1 red pepper, deseeded and thinly sliced**
- **1 roast chicken breast, sliced**
- **350g jar tomato and basil pasta sauce**
- **80g mature Cheddar cheese, grated**

1 Bring a large saucepan of salted water to the boil. Add the macaroni and cook according to pack instructions (10-12 minutes).

2 Preheat the oven to 190°C, fan oven 170°C, Gas Mark 5.

3 Drain the macaroni and mix it with the courgette, pepper, chicken and pasta sauce. Season with salt and pepper. Transfer to a baking dish and scatter the grated cheese on top. Bake for 30-35 minutes, until golden brown.

RECIPE AND FOOD STYLING: SUE ASHWORTH
PHOTOGRAPHY: JONATHAN SHORT

Brain Boosters

Kriss Kross

Try to fit all of the listed words back into the grid.

4 letters	5 letters	6 letters	7 letters	8 letters
DART	ATTAR	ARMFUL	BARRIER	BIGAMIST
HERD	INDIE	BOUNTY	CHIPPER	DESIGNER
ISLE	MINIM	CRITIC	TRAGEDY	NOISETTE
NAAN	NINNY	RESIDE	UNDRESS	PARAMOUR
		SAWYER		**13 letters**
		STEELY		REINSTATEMENT
				UNADULTERATED

Turn To Page 171 For Solutions

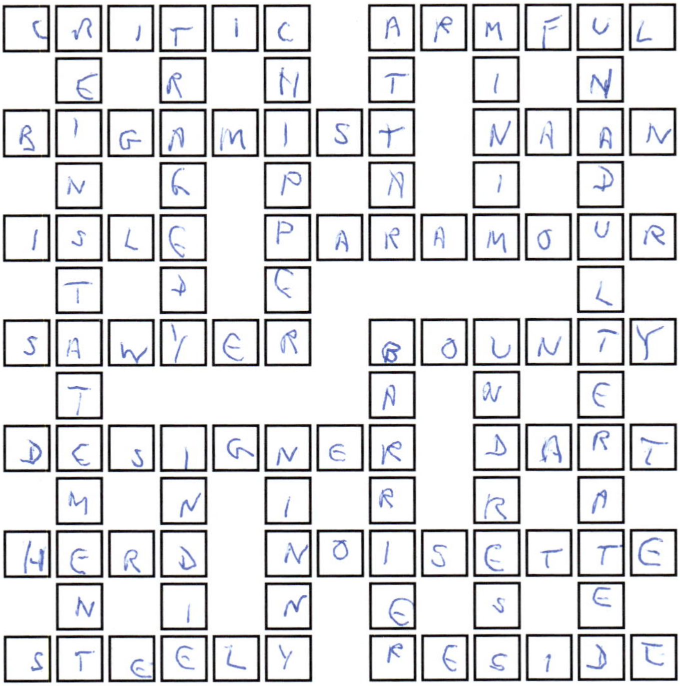

Sudoku

							5	
			9			2		
		6	5	3	4	9		
6	5			9				3
		1				7	2	
7	9			2				8
		4	2	8	5	1		
			1			8		
							3	

Fill in each of the blank squares with the numbers 1 to 9, so that each row, each column and each 3x3 cell contains all the numbers from 1 to 9.

Turn To Page 172 For Solutions

Word Wheel

You have ten minutes to find as many words as possible using the letters in the wheel. Each word must be three letters or more and contain the central letter. Use each letter once and no plurals, foreign words or proper nouns are allowed. There is at least one nine-letter word.

A Little May Day Magic

How many doors must would-be salesman Simon knock on before fortune smiles on him?

It was one of those jobs where you had to knock on doors. Simon wasn't keen, but the choice had been this or wear a floral garland and hand out leaflets in the square where the maypole was being erected for the May Day festivities. There weren't many holiday jobs for students this early in the season, and he really needed the money.

Staying in his lodgings saved travel costs too, although this was offset by having to feed himself all weekend instead of enjoying Mum's home cooking.

His mouth watered. *Don't think about that now.* Beans on toast were nutritious, even if you had them for every meal!

He opened a squeaky front gate and walked up a path littered with weeds.

There was movement behind the glass door. Then it inched open and an old lady with pink in her white hair, bright blue eyes, and coloured beaded chains around her neck regarded him suspiciously.

"If you're selling, you've come to the wrong house, dear. I'm not in the market for buying, and my scammer's budget has already been allocated for this quarter."

He was taken aback.

"I'm not a scammer. I promise."

"That's what the last one said." Behind her, a black and tan Alsatian padded along the hall and she stroked its head. "That's why I got Bruno. He eats scammers for breakfast."

"Um." Simon glanced at the dog, then back at the leaflet he was holding.

"My scammer's budget has already been allocated for this quarter"

The front door was in need of paint. This didn't look like a house whose owner could afford a new heat pump.

Although – he glanced at the leaflet in his hand – according to the sales hype you could save a fortune on your fuel bills if you got one installed.

He heard a dog bark gruffly inside. Hopefully it wouldn't come bounding out. He'd been wary of dogs since he'd been chased on his morning jog years ago.

"It's . . . well, it doesn't matter . . ."

"Not much of a salesman, are you?" She held out her hand. "You may as well show me since you're here."

Simon gave her the leaflet.

"It's a more economical form of heating. You can get government grants. They're more environmentally friendly."

"Huh. That's what they said about diesel cars when they wanted us to buy those." She handed the leaflet back. ›

PICTURES: DCT

"I hope you're not on commission, dear, because this estate is mostly pensioners, like me."

There was a direct challenge in her eyes and her lips quirked; he realised suddenly that she was enjoying this.

Emboldened, he said, "I thought you lot were the rich ones, what with the triple lock guarantee. It's us poor students who are living on baked beans."

"Nothing wrong with baked beans. I brought up my family on them." She laughed then. He'd been right about her enjoying it. "So are you at Exeter?"

"Yes, I'm doing computer science. This job's just to subsidise my grant."

"Well, good luck, dear. Try the Bluebell Estate – that's the moneyed end of town. You'll probably have more joy there."

She closed the door, not rudely but definitely firmly.

****

Bless him, thought Trudy Allsop, heading back into her kitchen. She did feel for students these days.

He'd looked startled when she mentioned she had brought up her family on baked beans. He'd probably have been open-mouthed if he'd known the full story. She smiled, remembering.

She'd been the bright one of the family. Destined to be the first to do higher education. She'd been so pleased and proud. But then she'd got pregnant.

At the time it had seemed like the end of the world. Her one chance of a better future, snatched away. She'd seriously considered giving up her baby for adoption and carrying on with her university plans. But when it had come to the crunch, she'd known she couldn't.

She'd loved the squalling, red-faced baby from the moment she was born. And motherhood had been brilliant. Especially as she'd been unable to have any more kids. Baby Alison was a one-off.

Trudy's fertility issues had been the cause of much heartbreak for a while. But when one door closes, another one always opens. Trudy was wise enough to appreciate that now.

****

Simon tried a few more doors on the Franklyn estate, but discovered Mrs Pink Hair had been right.

"You only have to sell one unit, and you'll be quids in . . ."

No one was interested in a heat pump.

She'd guessed right about him being on commission, too. It had seemed a good deal when he'd taken the job. As the manager of Heat Easy had said after his half-day training (also unpaid), "Lots of people will be home over the May Bank Holiday. You only have to sell one unit, and you'll be quids in."

Ho hum.

By late morning he'd decided to call it a day round here. Maybe he'd head over to the Bluebell Estate as Mrs Pink Hair had suggested. It made sense he'd find a customer in a place with more money.

****

Trudy Allsop had two granddaughters, Sophie and Belle, neither of them much older than the lad who'd come calling.

Sophie had gone to uni and now had a huge millstone of a loan around her neck, although it shouldn't be too long before she could pay it off. Sophie had always been a high-flier and she'd recently started her own company, which was doing really well.

Not that Trudy understood exactly what they did. It was the kind of job that hadn't even existed a decade ago. Something to do with diagnostics and portals and customer interface. It was online, of course, as the whole world seemed to be these days. Personally, Trudy still had a fondness for the old hands-on world.

Belle, her eldest grandchild, had got pregnant when she was just eighteen. Belle had always been more earth mother than career girl and little Freya, now six, was an absolute delight.

Trudy helped out with childcare. As did her daughter, Alison, when she wasn't working. And Aunt Sophie, when she wasn't slaving away online. With her gran, great-gran and auntie on the case, Freya didn't need expensive childcare. She was surrounded by love.

Trudy was just off to pick Freya and Belle up now. Then they'd collect Auntie Sophie who was having a rare day off, and the female side of the family were off to the bluebell woods at the back of the Bluebell Estate for a picnic.

Trudy called Bruno, and the big dog bounded eagerly down the hall.

****

Simon had a near miss at the first door he tried on the Bluebell Estate. The young couple said they were considering changing their heating system, and invited him in. He spent twenty minutes going through the ins and outs with them, and they seemed keen. But when they got to signing on the dotted line, the woman changed her mind.

"I'm ever so sorry. Your system looks really good, but we'd want to get more quotes before we made a final decision, wouldn't we, love?" She looked at her husband, who nodded.

"If you could leave all the information with us, we'll come back to you," he said.

"Great. Do you think that will be in the near future? Can I call back in a week?"

"More like a month, I'd say. We don't like to commit to anything until we've explored every avenue."

"Sure. I understand." Simon gave them a wide smile. It wasn't all bad news. He'd had a mug of fresh coffee and two chocolate biscuits.

As he left, the woman said, "You could try Annie at number seventy. She's been talking about heat pumps."

"Thanks. I will."

Annie greeted him warmly, but said unfortunately he was too late. She'd just bought one.

"A company called Heat Pumps R Us. I think they're on this estate somewhere, so they might have already done the rounds. Sorry."

Simon nodded despondently. Was it really worth continuing? The sky was a clear blue and there was a new spring warmth in the air. The kind of day he could have actually enjoyed. Not that he had anyone special to enjoy it with.

Maybe he'd just try a couple more houses.

He picked one at random. A cute little place in the older part of the estate with a red front door and a crazy paving path.

A hazel-eyed blonde not much older than him, wearing jeans and a T-shirt, answered the door. She was obviously surprised to see him.

"Oh, I was expecting my grandmother. Can I help you?"

"I'm hoping I can help you," he said with more confidence than he felt. "I'm calling to tell you about our range of heat pumps. Beat the winter fuel crisis."

"It's only May," she pointed out.

"Yes, but it pays to be prepared." Simon knew he sounded like a walnut. ›

He'd never been very confident around women. "There are grants available. I'd be happy to help with claiming one."

In truth, he was keen to carry on chatting – whatever it took. He was also aware of a car door slamming behind him.

"Sorry. I'm in a bit of a rush, but maybe I can take your leaflet." Her hand brushed his and he felt electricity fizz.

He bit his lip. He must be crazy. No doubt she was married to someone rich. This was a beautiful little cottage, and there was a newish BMW parked outside.

"Thanks anyway," he said. He couldn't push it. He turned away, and found himself face to face with Mrs Pink Hair.

"You again?" She grinned at him. "I see you took my advice, then?"

"You two know each other?" The girl looked between them.

"This young man called at my door this morning, and I suggested he try his luck over here. He's at Exeter," Mrs Pink Hair added, as if it were an explanation.

"Oh, I went there too." The blonde smiled. "What are you studying?"

"Computer science. I'm in third year."

"Same degree I did." She hesitated. "So this is your holiday job."

"It was this or wear flowers in my hair and hand out leaflets at the May Day celebrations."

"I'd have chosen this too. But I might be able to help you out. My company's always looking for temps. Have you heard of Tech Saturday?"

"Of course." Tech Saturday was one of Exeter Uni's success stories.

He was aware Mrs Pink Hair had retreated down the path.

"As I said, I'm just rushing off, but ring me. I'm Sophie Branning." She handed him a card. "My direct line's on there."

"Thanks so much. I'll call."

Simon's heart skipped a beat. It had more to do with the way their hands had touched again than the prospect of a job, although that was very exciting too. What an amazing coincidence that he'd knocked on her door.

****

Trudy was smiling as she drove Sophie, Belle and Freya into the car park that fronted the bluebell woods.

She was pleased the young man had called on her Sophie. He obviously had persistence and determination; traits Trudy admired. And if she wasn't mistaken, there'd been a spark between him and her granddaughter.

The scent of earthy dampness and bluebells filled the air

Sophie spent far too much time working – a possible romance would be good for her, she felt.

While Belle and Sophie got the picnic basket out, Freya chanted excitedly.

"*If you go down to the woods today, you're in for a big surprise*. Will there be a surprise today, Nanna Trudy?"

"We'll have to see," Trudy said, loving the expression on her great-granddaughter's face, and exchanging a glance with Belle and Sophie. The three of them had engineered a big surprise for Freya today, which had been a while in the planning.

Ten minutes later, having traversed a winding, dappled path through the papery white silver birches, they were deep in the heart of the bluebell woods. The scent of earthy dampness and bluebells filled the air. The flowers were at their peak and ›

the woodland was ablaze with a surreal blue light that looked as if dozens of fairies had daubed every delicate flower with some reflective paint.

"Isn't it stunning?" Belle murmured, as Freya skipped along the path with Bruno leading the way.

"Breathtaking," Sophie agreed.

"Turn left where the path forks."

Trudy called out a reminder.

A few moments later, the four of them reached the glade where a fallen moss-covered log made the perfect seat, although they'd also brought a fold-up chair for Trudy. It was harder getting up off the ground than it had once been.

Belle crouched down and whispered to Freya, "I think there must be fairies in this glade. Shall we have a look?"

Minutes later, Freya had found the first of the fairy doors. A tiny, hand-painted, blue door just like Trudy's real front door was half hidden in the shrubbery at the foot of a silver birch, in front of an arch fashioned by Mother Nature.

Freya squealed with excitement.

"Fairies *do* live here!"

"Not too loud, or we'll frighten them," Belle cautioned, smiling. "Shall we see if there are any more?"

The hunt began for the rest of the beautiful little doors that Belle and Trudy had been secretly making in Trudy's back room for the last few weeks.

Belle had inherited her talent for woodwork from her grandfather.

Trudy's late husband, Peter, had worked with wood all his life. He'd died a few years earlier, but Trudy had kept his workshop intact, and she and Belle had carried on making things using the techniques he'd taught them. It had felt like honouring his memory.

"Peter would have loved this," Trudy commented, while they watched Freya find more of the tiny doors, and the glade rang with stifled squeals of excitement.

"It's wonderful," Sophie said, eyes shining. "I'm so glad Belle's found her forte. She's so clever. There's definitely a market for these."

"When one door closes, another door opens," Trudy murmured. "Quite literally, in this case."

It was an expression Trudy had found to be true across the years. She'd had Alison so young she'd had plenty of time to revisit her education, but she never did, because she'd found something she'd enjoyed better.

Over the years she and Peter had fostered children, and even the more challenging ones had been a joy.

In the coming days, she planned to bring several of their fostered kids' offspring to picnic in the bluebell woods and see the fairy doors.

There was nothing like a touch of magic to give a child memories that would last forever. Creating happy memories of childhood were Trudy's speciality.

****

Not a million miles away from the bluebell woods, Simon had finally stopped for lunch. He still hadn't succeeded in making an actual sale, but he no longer cared about doors that weren't opened – or even the one that had been slammed in his face.

He turned the business card over in his hands. His heart beat faster just at the sight of Sophie Branning's name. He would phone her first thing tomorrow.

When one door closes, another door opens. That's what his gran had told him too. And suddenly Simon believed it.

The whole day, in fact the whole of his future, suddenly seemed alight with hope and optimism.

By Della Galton

Brain Boosters

Codeword

Each letter of the alphabet has been replaced by a number. The numbers for the first name of a celebrity are given. Work out which number represents which letter to reveal the person that Katie Boulter overtook in June 2023 to become the women's British No.1 tennis player.

■	18	25	12	22	4	5	22	22	8	■	18	2	13	2
6	■	12	■	9	■	18	■	9	■	18	■	21	■	24
5	20	22	12	19	■	17	22	21	9	7	■	2	23	24
17	■	22	■	5	■	26	■	■	■	17	■	20	■	12
5	20	11	5	18	19	■	18	3	23	17	26	26	17	26
17	■	9	■	■	■	18	■	9	■	19	■	9	■	17
■	26	8	17	26	■	25 K	2 A	19 T	12 I	17 E	■	20	2	20
9	■	■	■	9	■	12	■	19	■	18	■	■	■	19
15	12	2	■	7	2	12	15	17	■	19	5	18	25	■
17	■	21	■	20	■	20	■	23	■	■	■	9	■	9
23	17	26	17	18	12	13	20	■	18	7	12	10	17	26
18	■	9	■	12	■	■	■	3	■	23	■	23	■	26
17	22	1	■	14	17	21	23	2	■	12	23	2	19	17
22	■	17	■	17	■	12	■	22	■	20	■	20	■	23
22	2	20	26	■	18	19	23	9	20	13	21	9	16	■

A B C D E F G H I J K L M N O P Q R S T U V W X Y Z

1	2 A	3	4	5	6	7	8	9	10	11	12 I	13
14	15	16	17 E	18	19 T	20	21	22	23	24	25 K	26

17 E	1	1	2 A	

23	2 A	26	5	24	2 A	20	5

Turn To Page 172 For Solutions

May Day Emergency

A grand reunion garden party with dozens of cousins travelling from all directions . . . what could go wrong?

The idea of a grand family reunion had been discussed for a long time, with a variety of dates and locations suggested, before the majority of the relatives agreed that the ideal time would be the May Day Bank Holiday weekend.

It was the one public holiday of the year – apart from Christmas Day – that everyone seemed to be off work. Even better, the Monday itself was on May 4, otherwise known as *Star Wars* Day ("May the force be with you . . .") which delighted Ella's son, Tom.

"Let's have a *Star Wars*-themed party!" he begged. "I can dress up as Yoda!"

Ella laughed, then realised he was serious. She had thought he'd grown out of *Star Wars*, now he was twenty-five.

Ella and her husband, Dan, had three children, all in their twenties, with only Lucy, the youngest, still at home.

Cara, the oldest, worked about fifty miles away, so they saw less of her these days, which made Ella sad.

However, all three of the children were very keen to organise the family reunion. They had several uncles and aunts – both Ella and Dan were from large families – and multiple cousins, who were scattered all over the UK and beyond. Nowadays, they only really saw each other at weddings and funerals, and they all agreed that it would be nice to have a big get-together.

"We could have a garden party and put up a marquee!" said Lucy as the plan began to unfold. "The weather will be nice in May, and we can fit loads of people in – all the cousins can come!"

Ella frowned.

"When did we decide that the party would be at our house? I thought we'd only agreed on the date so far."

Dan looked up from his phone.

"Wait – what? A party here?"

Lucy jumped up and hugged him.

"Nice one, Dad! I knew you'd agree. Plus, it makes sense – we're the most central location out of all the family, close to all the motorways and the railway station, with easy access to the airport."

"When did you start working for an estate agent?" Tom joked.

Reluctant as she was to commit to hosting a party for thirty (even forty?) family members, Ella knew Lucy was right. If nothing else their home was accessible.

So with the decision on date and location reached, a message was posted on the extended family WhatsApp group, and the party planning began in earnest.

Cara was home the following weekend and mentioned that her friend, Darcy, had bought a marquee recently.

Ella was bemused to hear this.

"Why did Darcy buy a marquee? Does she regularly host weddings?"

Cara shrugged.

PICTURES: DCT

"It's more an extra-large gazebo. It's handy for get-togethers. Darcy's flat feels crowded with more than two people in it, but she has a decent-sized garden."

So a message was sent to Darcy, and the marquee/gazebo was booked for the first weekend in May.

"We could have the main party on Saturday, then brunch on the Sunday for anyone who stays over," Cara suggested, and all Ella could do was meekly agree.

****

As May drew closer, the logistics of the reunion seemed to be the only topic of conversation – who was travelling from where, with whom, and at what time. Lucy gave her mum an almost daily update.

"Auntie Jan and Uncle Bob are driving up on the Saturday and picking up Jade from university on the way," she said.

"Amy is flying in from Brussels and Uncle Mitch is collecting her at the airport. Sophie and Ethan are getting the train down, and Auntie Cath and the rest of the Cotswolds cousins are hiring a minibus and all driving up together!"

A party fund was set up, with everyone contributing a few pounds to cover the cost of food, drink and decorations. Platters of sandwiches were ordered along with prosecco, and ingredients to make a limited but potent selection of cocktails.

Cara was planning to bring the marquee to the house on the Friday, so they could assemble it the night before – "I'm not saying you're incapable, Dad, but there will be errors we'll need time to fix" – then decorate on the Saturday morning.

Which just left the tricky issue of what to wear. Ella had randomly decided to buy a jumpsuit after seeing one worn by the lead character in a drama she'd watched on TV – sophisticated and a bit more stylish than a dress – and Lucy had persuaded her that the occasion called out for professional hair and beauty input.

"Mum, your sisters will be here, and you can bet they'll be going all-out to look glamorous. I say we fight fire with fire!"

Lucy was right, of course. Despite them all being in their fifties, the sisters retained the competitiveness that had marked their teenage years. Ella appreciated her daughter's concern.

"We could get my friend, Skye, to do our hair and make-up on the Saturday," Lucy suggested. "That way we'll both look amazing for the guests arriving!"

And so Skye was booked.

"We'll decorate the gazebo and the garden in the morning," Ella said. "Then we can pick up the food and drink on the way back from Skye's."

****

With everything else booked, planned and organised, all that was left was to keep an eye on the weather forecast.

"Isn't it always sunny on the May Bank Holiday weekend?" Dan said as the date approached. "I'm pretty sure we'll be OK."

Ella loved her husband's optimism and when Cara arrived after work on the Friday before the party, the sun was shining.

"Let's get this thing put up in the garden, then we can maybe pick up some takeaway food and wine and get the party started!" Cara suggested, as she lugged a large box out into the garden.

She assured the rest of the family that she'd helped Darcy set up the gazebo two or three times (how many parties did the girl have? Ella wondered) .

They emptied the box and stood staring at the pile of steel poles, tent pegs, straps and sheets of plastic.

"It's much easier than you'd think," Cara stated confidently, as she began to separate the poles into groups depending on their size. "I'll read out the instructions and you lot do exactly as I tell you."

It took them less than an hour to get the gazebo up. They stared at it in awe.

"It's pretty big," said Tom. "It takes up most of the garden!"

"Perfect for a party," added Lucy.

"Reminds me of our holidays when you were children," said Dan fondly. "Anyone fancy camping out in it overnight?"

Ella quickly changed the subject. "Pizza, everyone?"

****

They all got up early the next morning and spent a couple of hours hanging bunting and making paper pompoms. When they'd finished, the whole space was a riot of colour. Apart from the sky, which had turned an ominous dark grey.

"I'm sure it'll blow over for when the guests arrive this afternoon," said Dan.

Ella and the girls left to get their hair and make-up done, and by the time they were done at Skye's house, with long, glossy curls and beautifully made-up faces, the wind was picking up.

Half an hour later, it was pouring rain and blowing a gale. They stared out of the window in horror, watching the pompoms turn to rainbow-coloured mush.

"Hate to say it, guys," said Tom, now fully dressed as Yoda, "but I think there's a danger the gazebo might take off."

It was true. The side panels of the structure were billowing outwards, like giant sails, and were being pulled upwards by the strength of the gusts.

"We can't risk it blowing away!" shrieked Cara. "Darcy needs it for her cocktail party next weekend!"

"No need to panic," Dan said, a slight note of hysteria in his voice. "We just need to hold it down and use duct tape to strengthen the joins!"

They opened the back door – the full force of the wind almost blew it off its hinges – and ran out into the garden.

It took seconds for Ella's stunningly styled hair to be transformed into a soaking mop. She could have wept, but there was no point as her face was already soaked in rain.

Between the five of them, they held the gazebo's poles and fought against the wind to stop the whole thing taking off.

"I made sure I hammered in the tent pegs really hard!" Dan yelled above the noise of the wind. "I'm sure the guy ropes will keep the structure tied down!"

With excellent comic timing, the tent pegs began pinging out of the ground, dragged by the force of the wind pulling the gazebo panels.

"We need to take the panels off!" Cara screamed. "They're acting like sails – there's no way we can hold this down!"

Tom and Lucy ran around the gazebo, untying the panels from the poles, and desperately folding them up to stop them taking off. As they removed the sheets of plastic on the roof, the decorations inside the structure blew up as though fired from a cannon and before long, the neighbours' gardens were covered in bunting and streamers.

Fifteen minutes later, the gazebo was dismantled and the family were back in the kitchen, with water pouring off them and make-up running down their faces (including Tom's, which he had painted full-on Yoda green).

As they sat in a bedraggled group at the table, their phones started pinging with updates from the family group chat.

Cousin Amy's plane from Brussels had been diverted due to high winds, meaning Uncle Mitch was waiting to collect her at the wrong airport.

The minibus with all the family from the Cotswolds had got a puncture on the motorway and the recovery truck was taking hours to get to them, due to the high volume of bank holiday weekend › traffic. Sophie and Ethan's train was stopped somewhere near Durham and could go no further due to a tree blown down on the line.

Uncle Bob had some kind of stomach bug and had been throwing up since first thing in the morning. He was the only one in the family who could drive, meaning Auntie Jan and Jade were also stranded.

As Lucy read each message aloud, her voice getting more and more hysterical, Ella started laughing. It was ridiculous – when was the last time there had been a near hurricane in the UK in May?

Dan shrugged.

"Ah well, the best-laid plans," he said. "Who's for a glass of Prosecco?"

****

They opened one of the platters of sandwiches and a big bag of fancy crisps, then popped the cork on a nicely chilled bottle of bubbly.

As they all laughed and chattered and ate and drank, Ella looked around at her little family and smiled. It might not be quite the reunion they'd been hoping for, but it would do for her.

"Ah well. I suppose I can return that jumpsuit I bought – it still has the tags on it," she said after having a long sip of delicious Prosecco.

"I might still put on my party dress," Lucy announced. "When will I get chance to wear a sequinned minidress again?"

"Sequins for a summer party? Isn't that a bit much?" Tom laughed.

"Seriously? Fashion advice from a man dressed as a kids' cartoon character?"

Tom looked hurt and offended.

"*Star Wars* is NOT a children's cartoon – it's possibly the greatest series in cinematic history!"

The family guffawed as Tom attempted to explain the hidden meanings and allegorical wisdom of his favourite film.

****

An hour later, as they finished their second bottle of Prosecco, they heard the front door opening and the unmistakable voice of Auntie Cath.

"Hello! We're here!" she called, before bursting into the kitchen, followed by about a dozen cousins. They were all immaculately dressed – it was like watching a catwalk at London Fashion Week as they trooped in.

"A friendly van driver stopped on the motorway and fixed our puncture for us!" Cath told them. "Plus Amy's flight has landed and she's on her way here in a taxi! And Sophie and Ethan were able to get off their train and on to a bus, and Uncle Bob is feeling a lot better so they're on their way up as well!"

Cath paused for breath and took in the sight before her – Ella, Lucy and Cara with their hair a mess and make-up all down their faces; Dan still in his pyjamas; Tom wearing a Yoda outfit with green paint smeared over his cheeks, and the table covered in glasses of Prosecco and half-eaten sandwiches.

"Looks like we arrived just in time!" Cath said with a grin. "Let's get a fresh bottle opened!"

And though it was a bit of a tight squeeze with such a crowd in the kitchen, they were all delighted to see each other and chattered away excitedly.

Ella laughed and hugged her sister, knowing she'd lost today's beauty contest, but just happy to be a part of this family.

Dan glanced out of the window as he uncorked another bottle.

"I think the rain's off and the sun might be coming out," he said. "Shall we get the gazebo back up?"

All things considered, it was shaping up to be a great weekend.

By Marie Penman

Brain Boosters

Kriss Kross

Try to fit all of the listed words back into the grid.

3 letters
ADO
ASS
EAR
ELF
ION
LEA
PLY
ROB
ROT
WHO

4 letters
ANTE
BEAM
CEDE
CULL
EPIC
ROMP
TUFT
YAWL

5 letters
HERON
METAL
MOLAR
SPOOR
THEIR
TOTEM

6 letters
DEDUCT
DORMER
ENTOMB
MOHAIR
SWATHE
THRONE

7 letters
BLENDER
DEMIGOD
HABITAT
LANTERN
OUTFLOW
SKETCHY
TWEETER
UNEQUAL

Turn To Page 172 For Solutions

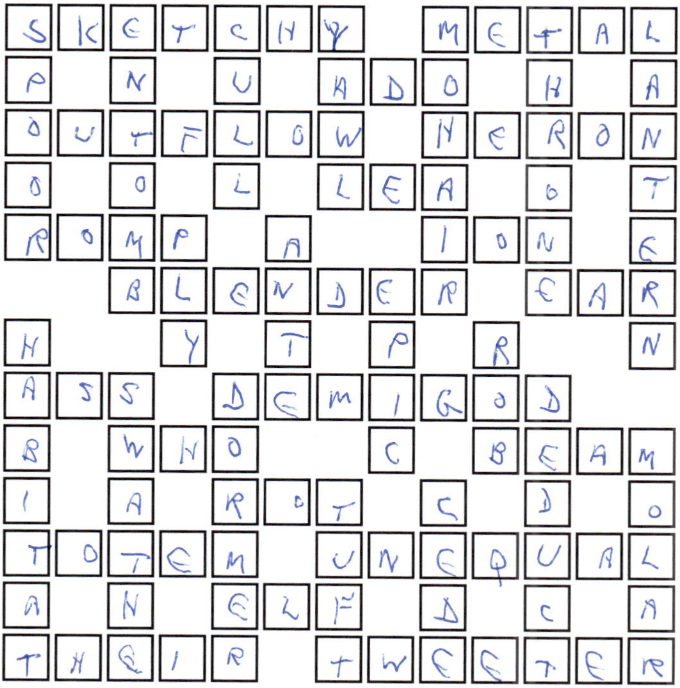

Food Fights

Their mother knew how the sisters annoyed each other – so why had she insisted they all holiday together?

They were six hours into their holiday before Lara first thought, *I don't think I can take two weeks of this,* and they were ten hours in before Jessie said it aloud.

"Don't be silly," their mother had answered placidly. "You're just sleep-deprived. The delay at the airport; the long drive. It'll be fine."

That was fair. The journey had been an awkward and disrupted one, though not very long, and they'd arrived in Spain at 2am. Their boys had been fractious and there had been inevitable fights over who got which room in the villa.

Toby, who was seven, wanted to jump into the pool straight away.

She gathered Zach and Toby in for a squeezy hug, making them giggle.

Lara caught Jessie rolling her eyes. Still, neither of them argued with their mother. Spending time together was the one condition Carmen had imposed when she'd booked the holiday.

So they went to the market, promising Toby they would all have burgers on the beach another day.

Lara was delighted by the market, and planned to come every day to buy ingredients for any meals they had in the villa. She could feel the fatigue sliding away from her in the warm sun, in the air on her bare arms, as she explored.

"Maybe you should have worn proper shoes instead of flip-flops"

Zach, who was fourteen, actually did.

Jessie just sucked her cheeks, disapproval written all over her face.

Carmen was unfazed, too busy marvelling over the welcome basket and complementary non-alcoholic wine.

It was lunch that finally cracked Lara, though. Toby wanted a burger on the beach. Lara and Zach wanted to go for a stroll and find some street food.

"That's fine. We'll just go our separate ways and meet up later, then," Lara suggested, privately loving the idea of a break from her sister.

"Nope," Carmen said. "It's a family holiday, remember? We stay together. I want to be with my grandchildren."

Jessie, however, was complaining about the price of things, and, by the way, her feet hurt on the cobblestones – whose idea had it been to come this way (Lara's, of course)?

"I'm so sorry for paining your delicate feet," Lara said. "Maybe you should have worn proper shoes instead of flip-flops."

"You see?" Carmen was saying to Toby while her girls bickered. "This paella is amazing, isn't it?"

And from that day forward, Toby would eat nothing but paella until they went home. Along with ice cream, of course.

"Don't you think Toby should go easier on the ice cream?" Lara said to Jessie.

"He's on holiday," Jessie said, plainly ›

affronted that Lara should even mention her son's diet.

They were already in the middle of a different argument at that point about what to watch on TV that evening.

"Zach chose where we went today," Jessie said, "so Toby should get to choose what we watch."

The kids had been scrolling through films trying to decide, while Lara and Jessie cleaned up the kitchen.

The film Zach wanted to watch was too violent for Toby. Toby wanted a cartoon. Jessie seemed ready to go to war to defend his choice.

"Fine," Lara said. "I don't mind.

"I'll go to my room and read."

"Don't do that," Jessie said. "Mum wants us all together, remember?"

Lara sighed. Carmen was outside, drinking a gin and tonic by the pool.

"I didn't think there'd be quite so much emotional blackmail involved when I took up this invitation," she muttered.

To her surprise, Jessie grinned.

"It's like cousin Tommy's wedding all over again, isn't it?"

Lara laughed out loud. When Lara was thirteen, Carmen took up sewing, and she was so proud of the dresses she'd made them that neither had the heart to refuse to wear them. They'd spent the entire wedding hiding from the photographer, and ended up sitting under the top table eating cake and playing Uno.

That might have been the last time she and Jessie had spent any real time together. These days it was only short visits, or Christmases where there was such a big crowd that they were hardly ever alone. Jessie's husband, Dan, was usually there too, an ebullient presence effortlessly keeping everyone happy and entertained with top-ups to their drinks or a funny story. A human social lubricant, their dad had called him.

Dan was supposed to be here too, but a work crisis had kept him at home. They were all missing him this holiday.

Jessie always seemed to be in a better mood when he was around. Or not so quick to find fault with Lara, anyway.

"You always make the gin too strong," Jessie grumbled now, taking a sip of the drink Lara handed her.

"You always make it too weak," Lara countered, as she poured a glug of extra tonic into Jessie's glass.

"It's like cousin Tommy's wedding all over again, isn't it?"

Jessie dropped a sprig of lemon verbena she'd picked outside into Lara's glass. Lara's favourite bit.

****

Next it was a fight over the washing machine, and where the most appropriate place was to hang wet swimming costumes ("Not on the oven, Zach!").

"It's like being sixteen again," Lara muttered to her mother when they were ready to leave for the market. They were, as usual, waiting for Jessie.

"Isn't it?" Carmen agreed happily. "I did love having you two girls at home. I miss that, you know."

"Miss arguments over the bathroom and fights over who stole whose CD?"

"Yes." She signed nostalgically.

Lara grunted in disbelief and went in search of Jessie.

Jessie was on the phone.

"No, of course I don't mind," she was saying when Lara found her in the bedroom. "I know you have to work." She pulled a face at Lara. "I have to go," she said into the phone, "they're waiting to leave. I'll get Toby to call you later."

"Dan?" Lara asked sympathetically when Jessie hung up.

Jessie nodded.

Lara wanted to ask why she'd pretended she didn't mind that he wasn't here. Instead she pointed to Jessie's feet.

"You're wearing flip-flops again."

"I don't have anything else. I forgot my sandals and it's too hot for trainers."

Lara showed Jessie the sandals she'd brought from her room.

"Use these. They're new."

Jessie looked at her dubiously.

"We're still the same size, right?" Lara asked. She didn't add, *You know, from when you used to nick all my favourite shoes out of my wardrobe?*

"Thanks," Jessie said grudgingly, accepting the shoes.

****

"All right, girls," Carmen said the next morning, joining them at the pool. "Today it's my turn to pick where we go."

"Is this because we took half an hour to agree on which flavour pizza to get last night?" Lara enquired.

"No," Carmen said, smiling mysteriously. "It's because today is the day for my bucket list item."

Jessie exchanged a suspicious glance with Lara. "What is it?"

"It's a surprise. The boys know all about it, and Zach's going to take care of Toby while we're gone." She clapped her hands as she turned back to the villa. "Hurry up, we leave in ten minutes!"

"Probably a spa day," Jessie whispered, rolling her eyes.

Zach floated past on an inflatable.

"I wish I was coming," he called.

Not a spa day, then, Lara mused, watching Zach splash Toby, and Toby squeal with laughter. At least the boys were getting along.

"At least the boys are getting along," Jessie said aloud.

It was quite sweet actually, the way Zach had taken to looking out for Toby, and how Toby rewarded him with something like hero worship. As neither of them had siblings, this relationship was a new experience for them.

"Don't forget the insect repellent this time," Jessie said accusingly, as she moved to rub SPF on the part between Lara's shoulders that Lara couldn't reach.

Lara leaned forward to let her do it.

"That was meant to be your job."

****

Swimming costumes, Carmen had instructed. Under very casual clothes. Then, when they were on the bus, she handed them each a pair of goggles.

"Water park?" Lara guessed.

Jessie laughed.

"No wonder Zach was jealous."

"Mum, has it been your lifelong wish to go down a waterslide?"

"Do you think I've never been on a waterslide?" Carmen said haughtily.

After a moment she added, "Dan made me go on one at that holiday park a few years ago."

Of course he did.

Jessie sighed. "I wish Dan was here."

"Our company isn't good enough?" Lara teased. But secretly she thought it was nice that Jessie missed her husband.

"I don't think your dad was thrilled about going to a holiday park that year," Carmen said vaguely. "Not that he would have said so."

"No – you and Dad never argued, did you?" Lara noted.

"No," Carmen mused. "He wouldn't."

Jessie sighed, sinking into her seat. ›

"No – neither will Dan, actually," she conceded thoughtfully.

Eventually they arrived in the centre of town. There were crowds of people everywhere and the bus had to crawl through traffic. Lara read a large banner as they drove past it.

"What's La Tomatina?" she asked.

The woman in the seat in front of them turned round and gave her a look of great incredulity and amusement. Carmen laughed.

Yes – it was clear that Lara had no idea what she was in for.

****

Later, all Lara could remember clearly was standing in the huge, excited crowd in the square, and the trucks full of over-ripe, unusable tomatoes parked all around, people unloading them into heaps. And then her heart racing when the firework was set off to signify the start of the festival.

It was Carmen who threw the first squashed tomato.

After that it was a chaos of juice, muck, slipperiness and lots and lots of red. The feel of squishing the fruit between your fingers before you threw it; the sensation of it slipping down your back or sliding down your leg when someone threw one at you.

Random strangers dropping fruit on her from the windows above; her tipping handfuls of fruit onto others who were useless, giggling heaps amidst a sea of scarlet tomato juice.

The world's biggest food fight.

It lasted an hour.

A friendly local with a hosepipe washed them off before they got back on the bus. Still, the stench was as ripe as the tomatoes had been.

Carmen couldn't stop laughing.

"I can't believe it, Mum," Lara said. "I never knew you had it in you! I looked over at one point and there was a guy twice your size running away from you!"

"I had so much fun!"

Their mother was so excitable; she had never looked so much like Toby after he'd had too much ice cream.

"Thank you for coming with me," she added, putting a hand on each of her daughters' shoulders.

"I can't believe it, Mum," Lara said. "I never knew you had it in you!"

Lara shared a smile with Jessie.

Jessie had a chunk of tomato flesh in the shell of her ear. Lara was pretty sure that was her doing, when she'd given her sister a tomato juice hair rinse, just before Jessie got revenge by slipping one under Lara's collar.

She hadn't felt so satisfied, or laughed so much, in years.

"Was this really a bucket list item?" she asked Carmen. A giant food fight was the last thing she would ever have imagined her placid mother dreaming of.

"I wanted to come with your father the last time we were in Valencia, but he refused to participate," Carmen said. "He couldn't bear the idea of conflict of any kind, bless him. But it's fine to fight sometimes. It doesn't mean that you don't love each other, right?"

She picked a piece of tomato skin off her eyebrow with a wistful smile, and leaned her head against the window to watch the scenery pass.

"It can even be fun."

By Camilla Kelly

Brain Boosters

Sudoku

					9	8		
		5	6			1	7	
	4			1	8			
	6					5	8	
		2				4		
9		4					6	
6	3		9	4				
	1		7		3			9
							1	

Fill in each of the blank squares with the numbers 1 to 9, so that each row, each column and each 3x3 cell contains all the numbers from 1 to 9.

Turn To Page 172 For Solutions

Word Wheel

You have ten minutes to find as many words as possible using the letters in the wheel. Each word must be three letters or more and contain the central letter. Use each letter once and no plurals, foreign words or proper nouns are allowed. There is at least one nine-letter word.

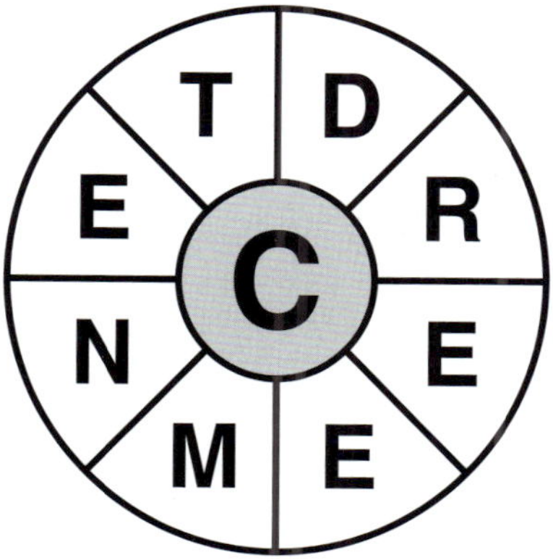

Frozen Summer Pudding

Ingredients (Serves 8-10)

- **500g frozen summer fruits, just defrosted**
- **50g icing sugar**
- **150ml whipping cream**
- **25g caster sugar**

For the centre:

- **200ml crème fraîche**
- **25g icing sugar**
- **200ml double cream**
- **2tbsp lemon curd**
- **Fresh summer fruits, to decorate**

1 Place a 1-litre bowl in the freezer to chill. Place the summer fruits in a food processor with the icing sugar and pulse to a purée. Pass through a sieve to remove the seeds. Measure out 300ml and chill the remainder.

2 Place the whipping cream in a bowl with the caster sugar and whip until it forms soft peaks. Fold in the 300ml fruit purée. Place in the freezer for an hour, or until it starts to freeze. Break up with a fork and transfer to the chilled bowl. Push around the sides to make an even layer, leaving the centre hollow. Freeze until firm.

3 To make the centre filling, place the crème fraîche in a bowl with the icing sugar and double cream and whip together until it forms soft peaks. Fold in the lemon curd. Transfer into the centre of the frozen ice cream and level the top. Freeze until firm.

4 To serve, dip the bowl briefly into hot water and turn out on to a chilled serving plate. Loosen the top edge of the pudding with a round bladed knife, if necessary. Decorate with fresh summer fruits and drizzle with the reserved fruit purée, if wished.

RECIPES AND FOOD STYLING: JENNIE SHAPTER PHOTOGRAPHY: JON WHITAKER

Brain Boosters

Codeword

Each letter of the alphabet has been replaced by a number. The numbers for the first name of a celebrity are given. Work out which number represents which letter to reveal the film that was directed by David Schwimmer and written by Simon Pegg.

17	10	9	17	18	16	21		5	25	18	12 D	25	18	24
	6		7		8		3		18		17 A		13	
17	13	14	17		16	14	13	10	20		15 V	21	14	7
	17		10		11		20		21		25 I		20	
16	11	13	21	11	21	10	10		14	17	12 D	25	13	10
	11		1				21		23				14	
11	8	14	21		21	18	20	14	21	18	16	26	21	12
			18		2				16		17			
4	3	10	20	10	16	14	25	4	20		10	26	17	26
	14				21		18				26		1	
26	25	16	16	13	4		7	25	7	11	25	16	17	11
	22		11		20		14		17		21		19	
9	25	11	3		25	12	21	17	11		14	13	25	18
	16		16		3		12		10		21		18	
5	21	21	9	21	18	12		7	17	18	12	17	24	21

A B C D E F G H I J K L M N O P Q R S T U V W X Y Z

1	2	3	4	5	6	7	8	9	10	11	12 D	13
14	15 V	16	17 A	18	19	20	21	22	23	24	25 I	26

14	13	18	,	22	17 A	20	7	3	8	,	14	13	18

Turn To Page 172 For Solutions

Kriss Kross

Try to fit all of the listed words back into the grid.

4 letters
HARE
ITEM
ORCA
SNOW

5 letters
ETHER
INTER
ROWDY
SOLVE

6 letters
ENTREE
LOCUST
PLAYER
RUSSET
STEPPE
UNPICK

7 letters
PROSAIC
SCHEMER
TWOSOME
UTENSIL

8 letters
FISHBOWL
MIGRAINE
OVERRIPE
TESTATOR

13 letters
PERSPICACIOUS
UNINTENTIONAL

Turn To Page 172 For Solutions

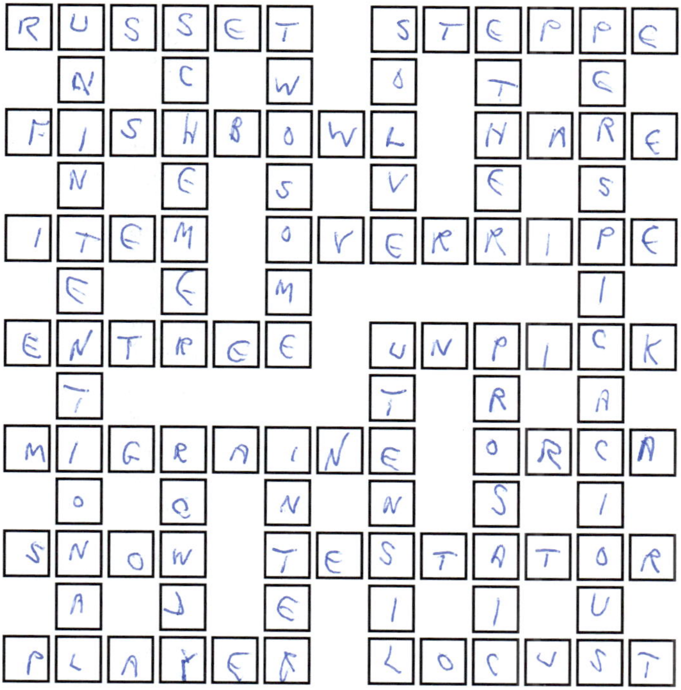

High Hopes

Evie was a fearless climber – but why did her confidence strike such dread into her mother's heart?

"Can I go on the climbing frame now, Mummy?" seven-year-old Evie asked as she leaped off the swing, her cheeks flushed from the cold wind.

Tasha smiled, pushing away the knot of anxiety in her chest.

"OK, sweetie."

Evie darted off, clambering up the equipment. Within moments, she was chatting to a boy around her own age.

"Let's go right to the top," she said with a giggle.

A man standing nearby, tall with a mop of dark brown hair, called out. "Ralph! Watch your footing, mate!"

Tasha's eyes met his. There was a slight tension in his expression, but his smile was warm.

"They make friends fast, don't they?" he remarked.

"They do," Tasha agreed, her gaze flicking to Evie, who was now swinging effortlessly from bar to bar. She drew in a breath and kept her face relaxed.

They stood in silence for a moment, then Glen said, "Ralph's usually a cautious sort of kid." His eyes followed his son as he climbed. "I only have him at weekends, so I suppose I'm hovering a bit more than I should." His smile didn't quite reach his eyes. "Last thing I want is my ex thinking I've been neglectful."

Tasha glanced at him, surprised by how easily he'd shared his feelings.

"Of course not."

She kept her tone light, but knew the pressure of trying to get things right.

"Does Evie have any siblings?" Glen asked, shifting the conversation.

"No, she doesn't," Tasha said. "It's just the two of us."

"Same with Ralph. Only child."

A sudden gust of wind made Tasha shiver, and she pulled her scarf tighter.

"Time to head home, now, Evie!" she called, watching her daughter give one last swing before dropping to the ground with a grin.

When Evie and Ralph both pleaded for hot chocolate she relented, laughing

"I'm Glen," he said. "That's my son, Ralph. Is that your daughter who's spurring him on?"

"Yes, that's Evie, and I'm Tasha."

She noticed the confident ease with which Evie moved.

Glen chuckled. "She's pretty fearless."

Like Brad, Tasha thought, a wave of sadness washing over her.

"How about a drink to warm us up before you head off?" Glen suggested.

Tasha hesitated, but when Evie and Ralph both pleaded for hot chocolate, she relented, laughing.

****

The local café was invitingly warm, filled with the aroma of fresh coffee. ›

IMAGES: DCT

They found a corner booth while Evie and Ralph sat at a nearby table, busy with crayons and paper.

"I hope I didn't come across as over-cautious back there," Glen said, sitting down opposite Tasha.

She smiled.

"Parenting is all about getting a balance, isn't it? You want to keep them safe, but at the same time, you want them to build confidence."

"Exactly," Glen replied, his shoulders relaxing slightly. "It seems like you've got it under control. You're calmer than me."

She shook her head.

"I'm just good at pretending."

For a moment, she wasn't sure why she was saying this.

"It's hard not to see what could go wrong. She loves gymnastics, climbing"

Maybe it was because he was a stranger – or because he understood what it was like to parent alone.

"Pretending?" Glen raised his eyebrows, curiosity in his expression.

"Evie's dad . . . Brad," Tasha began, her voice quieter now. "He died a year ago while rock climbing." Her throat tightened. "It was an accident; he wasn't being reckless."

Glen's breath caught.

"I'm so sorry," he said softly.

"I've tried not to let it affect how I parent, but when Evie climbs like that . . . it's hard not to see what could go wrong. She loves gymnastics, climbing – anything that gets her feet off the ground."

Glen nodded.

"It must be hard. Losing her father and then watching her being so carefree."

They talked for nearly half an hour, sharing their worries but also their pride in how resilient and spirited their children were, and the challenges of being a divorcee and a widow.

As they spoke, Tasha realised how proud Brad would be of their daughter's growing confidence.

Glen's eyes were kind, full of understanding.

"It must be tough with all the responsibility falling on you."

"Talking helps, though," she said, almost to herself, remembering an article about talking therapy she'd read in her magazine.

Glen nodded.

"Definitely. I've been muddling my way through lately."

Tasha finished her coffee and glanced at the time on her phone.

"Gosh, we'd better get going."

"Sure," Glen said, standing and reaching for his coat. "But if you ever want to meet up at the park again, I'd be happy to bring Ralph."

"That'd be nice," Tasha replied, exchanging numbers with him before heading out into the crisp air.

****

"What did you draw?" Tasha asked Evie as they left.

Evie held up a drawing of two figures beside a climbing frame.

"Me and my friend Ralph."

"Lovely," Tasha said. Evie had found a friend and perhaps, in a way, so had she.

Walking to the car, Tasha felt a lightness she hadn't felt in a long time.

It was just a small step forward, but it was definitely a start.

By Claire Buckle

Brain Boosters

Sudoku

			4				9	
					6		4	3
				5				
2				1			6	9
		4	5			7		1
	9							
				7		2		5
7	3		2				8	
	5		9	4		3		

Fill in each of the blank squares with the numbers 1 to 9, so that each row, each column and each 3x3 cell contains all the numbers from 1 to 9.

Turn To Page 173 For Solutions

Word Wheel

You have ten minutes to find as many words as possible using the letters in the wheel. Each word must be three letters or more and contain the central letter. Use each letter once and no plurals, foreign words or proper nouns are allowed. There is at least one nine-letter word.

Checking Him Out

Many people and their shopping passed through Pandora's till, but only one could make her heart race

"If you don't start concentrating at school," the woman scolded, "you'll end up working on a checkout, like this lady."

"That's right." Panda put her fingers beside her head, like horns, and leaned across her conveyor belt. "This is where the bad people end up."

The child giggled, and her mum at least had the decency to go red.

"I'm sorry, I didn't mean . . ."

"Forget it." Panda good-naturedly bleeped the last items of shopping across the scanner. "That'll be £44.27."

"Stop thief! Stop thief!" the man intoned like a Dalek.

They both laughed.

He had only a few items of shopping. Panda scanned the last: a carton of brightly wrapped chocolates.

"They look nice," she remarked.

"Here, have one." He ripped open the lid and offered her the box.

"Oh, I couldn't!" Panda flushed.

"To make up for your last customer. I shouldn't eat them all myself, anyway."

"Well, all right, then. Thanks!"

Then, out of the blue, there he was, next in line at her checkout

The woman quickly tapped her card and pushed her trolley towards the exit, lecturing her daughter all the way.

"Some people, eh?"

It was Panda's next customer. She looked up and met a sympathetic smile from an unexpectedly good-looking man.

"I think some people forget there's a person sitting here," Panda said breezily. "They think it's an automated service."

"I'd rather be served by a person than use the self-service tills," the man replied.

"Something usually goes wrong and an assistant has to come over anyway."

"Unknown item in the bagging area," Panda said in a robot voice.

She picked one out and felt something flutter inside her as she met his smiling eyes.

Quickly remembering she had a job to do, she said, "That's £15.76."

Tapping his card, he took his receipt.

"See you again," he said.

Panda wondered if she caught the hint of a wink before he turned away and disappeared into the crowd.

She didn't have long to think about it. Her next customer had a whole conveyor belt of groceries to scan.

The whole of humanity seemed to pass through the checkouts in the enormous supermarket where Panda worked. ›

PICTURES: DCT

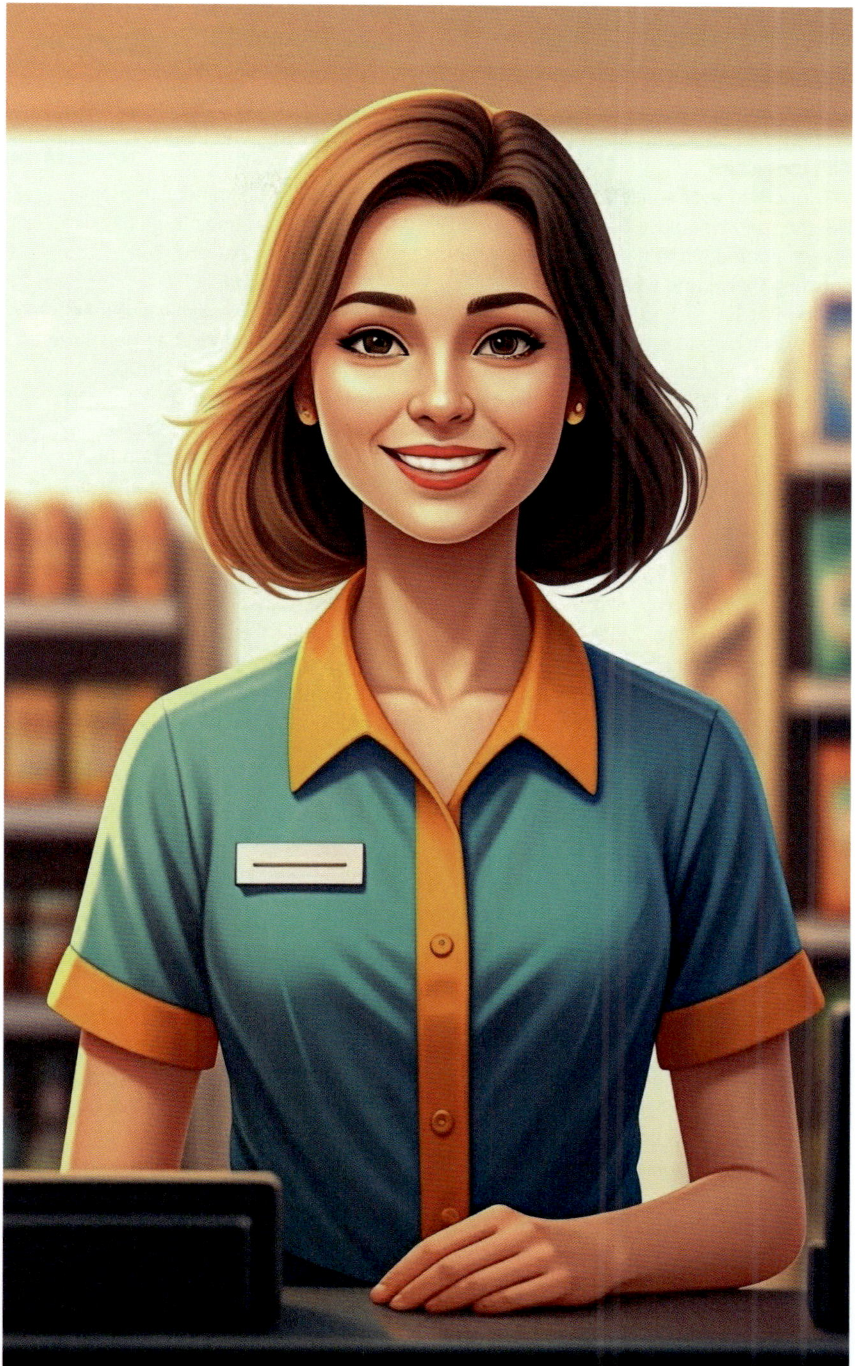

Some were chatty, some barely seemed to see her.

Most were simply polite as they packed their shopping, keen to get on with their day.

None had ever stuck in Panda's mind like the man who gave her the sweet. She wondered if she'd imagined the spark between them, and whether she'd ever see him again.

It was a big store beside a bypass, not the sort of local shop where you saw the same faces all the time. After a few days, Panda forgot about him.

Then, out of the blue, there he was, next in line at her checkout.

Bachelor shopping, she couldn't help thinking – just enough for a few meals

Heart quickening like a schoolgirl, she tried to think of something to say.

"Hello again," the man beamed. "How are you today?"

"I'm meant to ask that." Panda giggled. She began scanning and realised that he had once again bought very little, which meant she wouldn't have long in his company.

"No chocolates today?" she observed.

"If I'd known you'd be serving, I'd have bought some."

"I didn't mean I was expecting any!" she laughed.

"I'm still eating the last lot. I try not to have many, but I've got a sweet tooth."

"I know what you mean," said Panda. "I try not to keep sweets in the house in case I eat the lot."

He put his head on one side.

"I've never met a Panda before."

Briefly surprised, Panda remembered she was wearing a name badge.

"It's short for Pandora. Mum was an Adrian Mole fan."

"What an amazing coincidence – my name is Adrian."

"No way. Really?" Panda gasped.

"Just kidding," he laughed. "I'm Tony."

He held out his hand with mock formality. Panda shook it, giddily.

"Pleased to meet you, Tony."

"And you, Panda."

"Well, er . . ." Realising she'd held his hand a moment longer than necessary, Panda flushed. "That's £18.50."

He tapped his card.

"I'll remember the chocolates next time." He winked and went on his way.

Panda turned and gazed after his departing back until an impatient throat-clearing reminded her that she had a queue to serve.

****

The following week, Panda was enjoying a rare lull, with no one at her checkout, when she spotted Tony walking along the line of tills towards her.

He'd passed a couple of free checkouts and had obviously chosen to be served by her!

Sitting up straight, she pulled her lips into a pearly smile.

Her face fell as another man appeared from nowhere and pushed a piled-high trolley up to her conveyor belt.

Tony gave her a smile and a small wave as he walked on.

Panda didn't blame him for not wanting to queue. He only had a few items in a basket. But she wished he had waited. It would have been a clear sign that he wanted to talk to her again, as much as she longed to talk with him.

He'd seemed so flirty the last time they'd met. With a sigh, she concluded that he wasn't bothered about building on the connection they'd made.

When she'd finished checking out her customer's mountain of shopping, she spun round in her chair and gazed anxiously down the length of the store. But Tony was long gone.

Panda didn't see him the next week. It was her turn on the morning shift and Tony always seemed to shop in the early evening, as if on his way home from work.

Bachelor shopping, she couldn't help thinking – just enough for a few meals for one. He'd mentioned eating his chocolates by himself. She'd also checked that he wasn't wearing a ring. She felt certain he was single.

She wondered what he did for a living. His clean but casual clothes gave no clue. Panda told herself to stop obsessing over him. They'd got on well for a few minutes, and that was all.

It happened like that, sometimes, with men and women, young and old. Either she or a customer would utter a random remark that unexpectedly struck a chord. Suddenly they'd be chatting like old friends, even though they'd never met before and often never would again.

Such moments made Panda's job fun.

She couldn't help thinking that there had been more than that with Tony, though. He'd given her tingles that she'd never felt on a date – and she hadn't been able to stop thinking about him.

Surely he wouldn't have told her his name if he wasn't interested? Or was he just friendly and playful with everyone? It was so frustrating not knowing when, or if, she would see him again.

Back on the evening shift, Panda constantly scanned the tide of customers surging through the checkouts, hoping for a glimpse of Tony.

Pulse quickening, she saw him . . . at a checkout four in front of hers.

She felt rejected that he hadn't chosen her till, although she knew that was silly. The store was particularly busy and he'd obviously gone to the first checkout with a short queue – as any shopper would. He probably hadn't even seen her.

Panda struggled to keep him in sight through the gaps in the shoppers at the tills in between them. He was being served by Sophie, a particularly good-looking blonde, as cruel fate would have it. Jealousy stabbed Panda like a knife when they appeared to share a laugh.

As Tony started to walk towards her, on his way to the exit, Panda stared hot-cheeked at the goods she was scanning. She was determined not to look up at him. If he hadn't noticed her, she didn't want to look like she'd noticed him!

She couldn't resist a tiny, self-conscious glance.

"Evening, Panda!" He tossed her a heart-melting smile.

"Oh, hi, Tony!"

She wished he would stop for a chat, although she was too busy to pause her work. She had a mile-long queue.

Tony, in any case, didn't break his stride. He just passed by, out of her sight.

****

Over the next few days, Panda kept replaying Tony's "Evening, Panda!" in her mind. She was flattered that he'd remembered her name and taken the time to acknowledge her.

Perhaps he'd seen how busy she was and that was why he hadn't paused to say more. That was considerate of him.

On the other hand, she couldn't avoid the depressing feeling that she had been demoted from the Flirty Zone to the Nodding Acquaintance Zone.

Panda couldn't believe how many ›

times her spirits had swung up and down since she had first spoken to Tony.

It was like being on a rollercoaster, and utterly maddening – like being in love with someone who she didn't even know. Or was that exactly what it was?

****

Their next encounter caught Panda off guard. She was facing away from the conveyor belt, waving off a particularly chatty older lady who she had a good chinwag with most weeks.

Buoyed by their breathless exchange of news, she turned with a satisfied smile to greet her next customer . . . and it was Tony. Where had he sprung from?

"Hello, Panda, how's it going?"

"Good!" she squeaked. "You?"

"Great."

Scanning his first item, Panda racked her brain for something interesting to say. For days, she'd fantasised about conversations with Tony in which flirty banter zinged back and forth across the conveyor belt. She'd rehearsed frothy lines in her head, with every scenario leading to him asking her out – or even her asking him out. Now, caught on the spot, her mind was blank!

Searching for inspiration, Panda glanced at the car park, through the huge glass wall at the front of the store.

"The weather's a bit better today."

She kicked herself. The weather was one of the lame topics she discussed with every Joe Schmoe who passed through her checkout – not someone she was trying to find a connection with. Where had her fantasy romcom dialogue gone?

"Makes a change," Tony agreed.

"Have you had a good day?" she croaked through a parched throat.

"Oh, just work," answered Tony, packing his shopping. Panda wished he would elaborate, but it wasn't part of her job to pump her customers for information that they hadn't volunteered freely.

"Have you been up to anything interesting lately?" Tony asked.

His engaged tone made her look up.

"I, er . . ." His eyes were so mesmerising that she could only mumble, ". . .can't think of anything."

Dipping her gaze, she scanned another item and realised that it was his last.

"Um . . . that will be £19.68 please."

He tapped his card.

"Bye then."

"Yes, bye."

For the rest of her shift and long after, Panda cursed herself for making such a hash of things.

His question about what she'd been up to had been the perfect opening to tell him about one of her many hobbies and interests, and show she was more than just a checkout girl with a funny name. He, meanwhile, had brushed aside the opportunity to tell her anything about his work or give her a glimpse into his day.

Lying in bed that night, unable to sleep, She wondered how she'd let things slip backwards from flirting to nodding acquaintances to awkward strangers. For all her romantic fantasies, they were just a customer and assistant with nothing to say to each other.

What planet had she been living on?

****

Panda felt even more sorry for herself the following week, as she sat in a dentist's waiting room, cupping her cheek with her hand. She'd been daydreaming about Tony when she'd bitten into a carrot and snapped off half a tooth.

On a carrot of all things!

She consoled herself that at least she'd had one stroke of luck. She wasn't registered with a dentist because every practice in her area had a horrendous ›

waiting list. Despairing of getting her tooth looked at, she'd called 111 and been surprised to learn of a practice two towns away that offered emergency NHS treatment and got one of the limited slots available.

She'd phoned on the dot of eight and jumped with joy when they booked her in for two that day.

"Miss Green?" A smiley nurse called her name. "Dr Davis will see you now."

Heart drumming, Panda followed the nurse into the surgery and stopped.

"Tony!" she blurted.

"Hello, Panda." Tony rose, in pale blue scrubs. "When I saw the name I wondered . . . well, I thought there probably aren't many Pandoras about. Take a seat and tell me what the problem is."

Lying on her back, Panda didn't know what was making her heart race more, her usual fear of drills and injections, or the unexpectedly intimate experience of Tony's face leaning over hers while his gentle fingers explored her mouth.

His voice was so reassuring that his painless reconstruction of her tooth became an almost relaxing experience.

"There, good as new," Tony smiled at last. "Just stay away from carrots and stick to chocolates. Actually, don't tell anyone I said that."

"Thank you so much." Panda gazed at him with gratitude.

"Well, I guess I'll see you in the supermarket." Tony opened the door.

Despite his warm smile, she had the feeling she was being dismissed.

"I hope so."

Avoiding his eyes, she scurried out.

****

That evening, Panda admired Tony's handiwork in the mirror. He'd done such a good job that she couldn't tell the repaired tooth from its neighbours.

His skill and gentleness had made her fall in love with him all over again.

But although her tooth didn't hurt, her heart did. The briskly professional way he'd shown her out left no doubt that he had no intention of becoming more than an acquaintance. And why would he? A dentist and a checkout girl? She had to face it – he was out of her league.

****

On her day off, Panda went into the town square. She usually shopped in the supermarket where she worked after her shift. But when she only needed a couple of bits it was quicker to pop to the Co-op.

As she left, a voice said, "You'll be in trouble, shopping in a rival store."

"Tony!"

"Hello, Panda. Day off?"

"Yes. You?"

"Yeah. Do you have time for a coffee?"

"I'd love one!"

A few minutes later, they were sitting with cappuccinos. Panda couldn't believe how easily the conversation was flowing. They had so much in common!

"I'm so glad I bumped into you on neutral ground," Tony said. "I always wanted to ask you out, but I didn't want to hit on you at the checkout in case it embarrassed you – or you called security! I couldn't ask out a patient, either. Luckily that was a one-off and you're not registered with me."

"Then here's to neutral ground!" Panda raised her cup and clinked it with his.

"Does that mean you'll come out with me again?" Tony's eyes shone hopefully.

"I'd love to."

As they left the coffee shop, Tony said, "You know, we'll have a great story when people ask how we met. I'll say you kept checking me out in the supermarket!"

By Julia Douglas

Brain Boosters

Codeword

Each letter of the alphabet has been replaced by a number. The numbers for the first name of a celebrity are given. Work out which number represents which letter to reveal which 2013 song was a collaboration between Brian May, Slash and David Attenborough.

■	13	18	19	14	■	13	3	26	9	■	6	16	18	21
13	■	7	■	25	■	10	■	19	■	17	■	3	■	18
18	2	3	9	19	■	9	■	18	9	2	1	4	18	20
2	■	2	■	17	12	26	25	8	■	18	■	■	■	18
21	19	18	7	10	■	17	■	18	25	9	16	3	2	21
18	■	22	■	19	■	10	■	11	■	2	■	26	■	■
14	9	3	14	14	20	■	23	10	23	10	19	11	3	■
10	■	■	26	■	■	10	■	22	■	■	25	■	■	8
■	2	3	19	11	10	5	11	■	16	10	11	1	18	16
■	■	4	■	9	■	13	■	24	■	19	■	10	■	25
8 B	10	16	25	10	7	10	■	10	■	6	10	18	17	11
9 R	■	■	■	19	■	2	26	9	25	3	■	16	■	15
25 I	16	16	25	2	25	11	■	17	■	9	18	25	17	10
18 A	■	18	■	1	■	10	■	10	■	2	■	19	■	22
19 N	10	4	17	■	25	22	16	20	■	10	22	14	20	■

A B C D E F G H I J K L M N O P Q R S T U V W X Y Z

1	2	3	4	5	6	7	8 B	9 R	10	11	12	13
14	15	16	17	18 A	19 N	20	21	22	23	24	25 I	26

8 B	18 A	22	14	10	9 R		17	4	18 A	14	14	10	9 R

Turn To Page 173 For Solutions

Dark Mushroom Tart With Crunchy Garlic Top

Ingredients (Serves 6-8)

- **350g shortcrust pastry (bought or homemade)**

For the mushroom filling

- **75g butter**
- **1 medium onion, finely sliced**
- **450g dark open-cup mushrooms, sliced finely grated zest and juice of 1 lemon**
- **1tbsp mixed dried herbs**
- **200ml double cream or crème fraîche**
- **3 large eggs, beaten**

For the garlic crunch topping

- **55g butter**
- **150g stale breadcrumbs**
- **3 garlic cloves, crushed or finely chopped**
- **3tbsp chopped fresh parsley**
- **salt and freshly ground black pepper**

1 Preheat the oven to 200°C/ Fan 180°C/ Gas 6. Roll out the pastry large enough to line a 24cm x 3.5cm deep tart tin. Line the tin and trim. Chill or freeze for 20 minutes, prick the base all over with a fork, then bake blind. Cool in the tin.

2 Melt the butter in a large frying pan, add the onion and fry until soft and golden. Add the mushrooms, lemon juice, herbs, salt and pepper to taste and fry over a medium-high heat for 5 minutes until the mushrooms are tender and all the liquid has evaporated. Cool slightly.

3 Make the topping. Melt the butter in a frying pan, add the breadcrumbs, garlic, lemon zest and parsley. Fry over a brisk heat for about 2-3 minutes until the breadcrumbs begin to crisp and turn golden – tip into a bowl to stop them cooking.

4 Beat the cream with the eggs and stir in the mushroom mixture. Pour into the pastry case, level the surface, and sprinkle the topping evenly over the top. Bake for 20-25 minutes until set, crisp and deep golden on top. Serve warm with a tomato salad and some salad leaves.

RECIPES AND STYLING: MAXINE CLARK PHOTOGRAPHY: LIGHTHOUSE

The Friend Zone

Would Henry's unspoken, wistful devotion to his lovely housemate ever be recognised?

Henry watched from the sofa as Daisy zipped up her black ankle boots, then pulled her bag over her shoulder.

She looked at herself in the mirror and frowned critically.

"Well," she said to him with a shrug. "I guess this'll have to do."

He wanted to tell her that he had never seen anyone look so beautiful. That the man, John, she was meeting for the first time would never be good enough for her. But he couldn't.

She looked at him affectionately. "Right, see you later. OK?"

The first time he'd set eyes on Daisy, it had been love at first sight. The woman at the agency who had found him the place had told him that Daisy was simply adorable.

And she was. She'd instantly put him at ease; made him feel welcome. They'd been best friends almost from the start.

Sometimes when they were sitting together on the sofa, or eating dinner together in the kitchen, he'd think to himself, *This is perfect.*

As long as they had each other, he didn't need anyone else.

It was always Henry who coaxed the first post break-up smile from her

Henry gave the briefest of nods. He couldn't tell her how much it broke his heart when she left the house they shared to go on a date, or talked about finding someone to spend her time with.

He wondered whether one day she'd turn to look at him with those beautiful brown eyes, and realise that her best friend, her housemate, the one she spent evenings chatting to on the sofa, or going for countryside walks with, or sitting companionably in the kitchen at breakfast time with, loved her more than anyone else ever could. That she didn't need to look for anyone else.

He was completely and utterly in love with her, would do anything in his power for her. But of course, he couldn't say anything.

He couldn't ask her why she continued to flick through those dating apps on her phone, looking for a man she wanted to spend her time with.

"Oh, Henry," she'd said to him once, giving him an affectionate hug. "Why can't I find a guy just like you?"

****

From time to time, she'd start a relationship. There would be a man in ›

IMAGES: DCT

their lives, sitting on the sofa, taking Daisy out for fancy dinners.

Then things would end; Henry would help her to dry her tears, encourage her out for a walk, or to spend some time on the beach nearby. It was always Henry who managed to coax the first post-break-up smile out of her.

Some of her boyfriends were OK. They'd talk to Henry, wouldn't mind him tagging along sometimes.

"After all," Daisy would tell them firmly, "he's my best friend."

Other boyfriends he disliked from the start. Their manner was always off.

He'd wait until Daisy was out of the room and then glare at them until they silently looked away.

But he'd never do anything more – he loved Daisy far too much to ever embarrass her or let her down.

****

The evening closed in. The TV flickered – an old football game was playing itself out. Henry felt himself getting sleepy.

Daisy didn't know it, but he always endeavoured to stay awake while she was out, just to make sure that she got back home safe and sound.

Sometimes she'd take a bus back, and walk the final hundred metres or so, and he was always worried about her safety.

Only when he heard the click of the key in the lock would he finally let sleep take him, no matter how late it was.

Tonight, she was later than usual – the cars that steadily made their way along the road thinned out and had almost disappeared as night fell.

Only the roar of on occasional bus or the sound of footsteps passing could be heard. Where could she be? Where had his precious Daisy got to?

And then, finally, it came – the click of the lock; the sound at which he usually let himself fall into slumber.

But something felt different tonight.

He heard her kicking off her ankle boots, and then rather than going straight upstairs to bed as she often would, she came into the living room.

She stood there in the half-light, the flicker of the TV lighting up her face intermittently.

"Oh, Henry," she said, clearly close to tears. "That was an absolute, unmitigated disaster! What a total waste of an evening!"

Something felt different tonight. He heard her kicking off her ankle boots

The restaurant had been awful, and her date had talked constantly about himself. They'd gone on to a bar afterwards, Daisy itching to get home but too polite to say so.

Then when she'd told her date that she'd rather not go home with him, he'd ordered a taxi for himself and disappeared, leaving her on her own.

Henry felt a flash of anger and indignation and leapt to his feet.

"That's right, Henry. I know if you'd been there you'd have let him have it!" she said with a smile, flopping down onto the sofa next to him and putting her arm around his back. "You're the best doggy in the world."

And then he relaxed and snuggled up to her. Because once again it was just Henry and Daisy, Daisy and Henry. Just the way it should be.

By Gillian Harvey

Chocolate Orange Tiger Cake

Ingredients (Serves 12)

- **340g baking margarine**
- **340g caster sugar**
- **6 large eggs**
- **400g self-raising flour**
- **35g dark cocoa powder**
- **180ml milk**
- **1tsp natural orange extract**
- **Orange food colour gel**
- **200g orange buttercream icing**
- **200g orange ready to roll icing**
- **50g chocolate ready to roll icing**

1 Preheat the oven to 180°C, Fan Oven 160°C, Gas Mark 4. Grease and line 2 x 7cm deep 20cm round cake tins.

2 Use an electric whisk to gently mix the margarine, sugar, eggs and flour together, then continue to whisk until smooth and creamy. Divide between 2 bowls.

3 Add cocoa powder and 115ml milk to one bowl and orange flavour, colour gel and remaining milk to the other. Whisk each mixture to make 2 soft cake batters.

4 Spoon a large spoonful of the chocolate mix into the middle of each cake tin. Tap each tin on the work top to smooth the mixture. Place a spoonful of the orange mix on top and tap the tins again.

5 Continue adding alternate spoonfuls of cake mix directly on top of each other, tapping the tins to flatten the mixture each time.

6 Bake for 40-45 minutes until firm. Cool for 10 minutes, remove from the tins and cool on a wire rack.

7 Spread one cake with ¾ of the orange buttercream and position the other cake on top. Spread the top surface thinly with the remaining buttercream.

8 Roll out the orange icing to an 18cm round. Roll out the chocolate icing thinly and cut out stripes and flashes. Arrange on top of the orange icing and roll gently to smooth the surface. Cut out a neat 20cm diameter circle and place on top of the cake to serve.

RECIPES AND STYLING: KATHRYN H NS PHOTOGRAPHY: STUART MACGREGOR

Dog Person

Maybe I should have been completely honest with my new colleagues . . . but my brother's pal was happy to help

The problem with Take Your Dog to Work Day is that I'm a cat person. The second problem is that I'm the only one.

When I first started working at my new IT job in a team of six, I was extra keen to fit in, and so I guess I might have pretended more of an interest in Alison's labradoodle and Sam's three beagles than I actually felt.

So it wasn't really surprising when Alison assumed the whole group would be on board with the idea.

And it certainly wasn't her intention, I'm sure, to set off quite so much anxiety in me about it. After all, she knew I didn't have a dog of my own. And she thought – quite accurately – that I'd be fine having all their dogs around, seeing as they were all a friendly, well-behaved bunch – like a group of toddlers whose parents all knew each other from NCT classes.

caught in his mouth so dexterously that Mum applauded. Carl was a dog person.

"I just don't want to be left out," I said.

They knew it was a sore spot. I'd been made redundant from my last job, and although I knew logically it was because of cutbacks, part of me still wondered if things would be different if I'd spent more time at after-work drinks, conversing about football and video games.

It worked out well; I liked my new job with Alison's online craft business more. But that just made me desperate to do everything I could to keep it.

"Take a huge bag of treats and make all the dogs love you," Carl suggested.

"It's not as if you've got anything against dogs," Dad said, helping himself to extra gravy.

"You're very good with animals," Mum put in encouragingly.

"High strung," my brother tutted when I explained the situation to him

What she underestimated was how sensitive I'd be to the idea of being the odd one out. But how could she have known, given how hard I tried to hide it?

Neurotic and needy was not the impression I wanted to make on my new work colleagues.

"High strung," my brother tutted when I explained the situation to him over Sunday lunch at our parents' house. "Typical cat person."

I threw a sprout at him, which he

Carl burst out laughing. "Except the hamster we had that bit her finger every time she went near it. And the rabbit who ran away whenever it heard her voice."

"Come on. I was fine with Jasper's dog, wasn't I?" I said defensively.

Carl tilted his head thoughtfully, but even he couldn't deny that when he'd been dog-sitting for his friend Jasper and asked me to cover for half an hour while he went to a dental appointment he'd forgotten all about, that, yes, the dog had ›

PICTURES: DCT

been fine. It had survived and everything.

In fact, Ludo and I had bonded over our love of Carl's special breakfast granola. But I didn't tell Carl that.

Now, with the kind of flash of insight and brilliance that occasionally made me grateful he was my brother after all, he said, "Why don't you ask Jasper if you can borrow Ludo for the day?"

I liked the idea. Ludo had been a calm, low-maintenance greyhound, and having him there would mean that I could enter into all the conversations about biodegradable poop bags and the best walkie parks with my colleagues.

"Will Jasper be OK with it?"

"Probably. Jasper's very chill." He popped another sprout into his mouth, and said with a grin, "He's not a cat person."

I rolled my eyes.

"Would you ask him for me?"

"I'll see what I can do."

****

Carl had been friends with Jasper for years, since they'd met at some horrible-sounding fitness group where they did things like 5am runs up snowy hillsides, the appeal of which was a complete mystery to me.

Despite my having been aware of Jasper for a long time, we'd only met once or twice. I was pretty nervous when I arrived at his doorstep on Saturday afternoon.

He seemed to take forever to answer the door, and when he did, he was groggy and sleep-mussed, dressed in an old T-shirt and joggers.

"Oh. Sorry. I woke you up," I said, embarrassed on his behalf. It was mid-afternoon. I wasn't even early.

"Carl said to come at four o'clock . . ."

He frowned at me.

"It's Gabby, isn't it?"

In fairness, some people take a while to come around when they first wake up.

"That's right."

"What can I do for you?"

My heart sank as I realised what was happening. This time I was embarrassed on my own behalf.

"Carl hasn't spoken to you, has he?"

All these years and I still hadn't learned my lesson about my brother's notorious unreliability.

She was small for her breed, a pale dove-grey colour, with a wary head tilt

Jasper shook his head with an expression of sympathy that told me he knew exactly what Carl was like.

"Never mind," I said, backing away from the door. I was going to murder Carl. "Sorry to have bothered you."

"It's fine," he said. "What was Carl supposed to have spoken to me about?"

As I hesitated, Ludo came out of the room behind him, made a weaving path of the hallway, investigating all corners, and then came to stand beside Jasper. She was small for her breed, a pale dove-grey colour, with a wary head tilt.

"Um," I said. I was going to murder Carl. "It's going to sound a bit weird . . ."

I couldn't even back out because no doubt Jasper would ring Carl straight away and Carl would tell him everything anyway.

"We're having a bring-your-dog-to-work day next week and I was wondering if I could borrow Ludo."

His face was blank. Maybe he still wasn't fully awake.

"Carl suggested I should come over

this afternoon. I guess he knew you'd be home," I went on. "He was supposed to ask you about it, or of course I wouldn't have just shown up like this."

Jasper looked at Ludo. Ludo looked back at Jasper.

"I think she's fine with it," Jasper said, as if it happened all the time that near-strangers asked to borrow his dog. "Do you want to come in?"

He led me through to the kitchen, pointed out the kettle, the mugs, where the coffee was kept.

"Why don't you make us a drink while I get changed? We can take Ludo for a walk and the two of you can get used to each other," he said, before disappearing into his bedroom.

Ludo was staring at me.

"Hi, Ludo," I said, keeping my voice low so Jasper wouldn't hear me introducing myself to a dog. "I'm Gabby. Remember me?"

She kept staring at me. I crouched to her level and reached a hand out to her. She came closer for a sniff, then sat down and stared at me again.

"All right, then," I said after a moment, standing up again. "It's always fun to get two socially awkward people together."

****

Whatever the opposite of socially awkward was, that was Jasper. Not in the sense that he was polished and charming and well-mannered; more that nothing fazed him. He was so casual and easy that within minutes I felt there was no pressure to being in his company, and I actually started to relax.

I mean, when someone pulls a half-chewed dog biscuit out of his shoe before he puts it on, there doesn't seem to be any need to stand on ceremony with him.

Before we left, he took the two mugs of coffee I'd made and poured them into a Thermos, leaving just a little behind, which he glugged like a shot.

"Come on, Ludo. Let's go," he said, slipping the Thermos into his backpack.

She stayed seated, staring.

"Is it me?" I asked.

He seemed amused.

"Why would it be you?"

I shrugged. Could she tell I wasn't a dog person?

"It's the weather," he said. "She won't go out if it's raining."

He went to the front door and opened it. Ludo moved so she could see outside. It was cloudy, getting dark, but dry.

Agreeably, she came to him so he could put her lead on.

"She refuses to get her feet wet," Jasper explained.

"I'm the same!" I said, feeling sudden kinship with her.

I was also relieved. One of the things I'd worried about was having to deal with a muddy dog who loved running through puddles and piles of wet leaves. Katie told me she'd spent all last weekend cleaning her car after her dog jumped in the river.

Jasper smiled at me. I was getting used to that bemused expression whenever he looked at me.

"I didn't think that dogs were so particular," I said.

"This one is."

We finally left the house.

"There's a park around the corner," Jasper said, leading the way.

I nodded, watching Ludo. She was well trained, walking close beside Jasper with a light, graceful step.

"I got a retired greyhound thinking I'd have company on runs and training," he said. "Ludo wouldn't even come with me this morning when I went on a mud run."

"What's a mud run?"

"A 10k obstacle course. There's a lot of mud involved." ›

"Sounds horrific." I shuddered.

"You two have a lot in common. She waited in the car. In fairness, it was 7am. And she's more of a sprinter than for long distance. Actually, she's more of a cosying-up-in-front-the-fire type of dog."

I noticed another dog, a stately Alsatian, coming towards us with its owner. As it came nearer to us on the pavement, Ludo nervously fell to the other side of Jasper, sheltering herself between him and me.

"Were you disappointed?" I asked.

"Not at all." He put his hand out to pat Ludo reassuringly as the Alsatian sailed past, unconcerned.

I had already done the same, without even thinking, my heart going out to another shy creature, and so his hand covered mine momentarily.

I drew back, awkward all over again, but he just smiled and went on, "She may not be good company on an assault course, but she's the best to come home to. She always knows how I'm feeling, and when I need a hug."

Jasper didn't look to me like the kind of person who ever needed a hug. He was very tall, for a start.

"Do people who run assault courses ever need a hug?" I asked.

He laughed. "Never more than when they've done a mud run."

"That's why you were asleep when I arrived," I said apologetically.

"Yes. But let's blame Carl for that one, shall we?"

He grinned conspiratorially, and I was only too happy to join in.

When we arrived at the park, Jasper let Ludo off her lead, but she stayed close beside him as we walked. There were a few other dogs around – a black Labrador running about exactly like my five-year-old neighbour did after his mother let him have too many sweets, and two dogs making friends by sniffing one another while their owners chatted, partially blocking the path.

We walked through this section, along a tree-lined path into the next field.

Ludo began to perk up. Jasper unzipped his bag and pulled out a bright orange frisbee. But it wasn't until we emerged properly into the field and Ludo could see that we had it almost to ourselves that she began to get excited.

"Off you go, then!" Jasper said to her.

He threw the frisbee, and she was so fast she actually overtook it and had to wait for it to drop.

Ludo was back in seconds, having barely hit jogging speed. I tried again

Then she was back to us with the frisbee in her mouth, looking up at Jasper adoringly.

Jasper threw it a few more times, Ludo catching it every time.

"Do you want to take over while I pour the coffee?" he asked me.

I hesitated. I hadn't thrown a frisbee since I was nine years old.

"I won't be very good," I warned.

"She won't judge."

I took the frisbee, held it hesitantly while Ludo waited. Eventually, seeing Jasper's attention was on unpacking the Thermos, I made an attempt at throwing.

It was pretty feeble. Ludo was back in seconds, having barely hit jogging speed.

I tried again. Slightly better.

This wasn't so hard. You just needed to find the knack.

So I dedicated myself to finding the ›

knack: the right execution that satisfied me and Ludo, that made the frisbee fly.

I somehow found it. There was one throw that sailed out of my hand, and glided with heft and the breeze almost the full length of the field. Ludo was so delighted with it that she did a victory lap of the field to express her joy.

****

I didn't know how much time had passed. I was too absorbed in what I was doing. But when I turned to Jasper, he was sitting on the bench with an empty coffee cup, and the second cup had gone cold beside him.

He was smiling in that easy way of his, his bemusement suddenly looking more like appreciation.

My wrist ached, my shoulder burned, my face was numb with cold. But I almost felt I could have joined Ludo on her run around the field, I felt so energised.

"She's like a different dog," I said breathlessly.

"She's just being herself," he said.

Ludo returned to us – returned to me. When I reached to pet her, she pushed into my hands affectionately.

For the first time, I could see what the fuss was about dogs.

****

The plan was to pick her up early on Monday and spend some time with her before taking her to the office.

But when I stepped out of my house into sleeting rain that morning, I knew it wasn't going to happen. Instead, I arrived at work alone, and sat in my car for an extra minute trying to brace myself to face the rain. And the office.

My phone rang while I was bracing.

"Hi," Jasper said. "I got your text. Sorry we won't be seeing you today after all."

"I didn't have the heart to coax Ludo out in this weather," I said apologetically.

"Probably for the best. It might have taken all morning."

"And honestly," I said, "I thought perhaps she might not enjoy the company of so many strangers. She seems quite shy."

That was what had really changed my mind. I could almost hear him smiling.

"She's just fussy about who she spends time with. Very high standards."

Was that a compliment? My heart gave a little cheer.

"Thanks for letting me spend time with her," I said. "I'll miss her company today."

"You don't need to," he said. "If it stops raining later you could come by after work. Join us on our walk."

I scratched my nose, bit down a smile, squeezed the phone tighter.

"I'd like that."

"You can tell me all about how your day goes." It was weird how appealing I found that idea. "It might even be your chance to confess," he said.

"Confess?"

"To your colleagues. That you're not really a dog person."

So it had been obvious. To Jasper, at least. But the thing about Jasper was that I really didn't mind that he saw straight through me.

"I might do that," I murmured.

It was possible, I thought, as – fully braced – I walked into the office to greet my five colleagues and their eight dogs, that I could try to be a bit more authentic around my new work friends. Let them see the real me.

But it was also possible, I thought that afternoon – when Kevin's elderly spaniel came and put his head in my lap for a quiet siesta – that my real self, it turned out, actually quite liked dogs.

By Camilla Mohsen

Brain Boosters

Kriss Kross

Try to fit all of the listed words back into the grid.

3 letters
AGA
APT
BID
GAL
GIN
SIR
TON
URN
VIM
YEN

4 letters
BEAU
BOMB
ESPY
LIST
MENU
ORCA
PLEA
SEEP

5 letters
ATLAS
HIKER
IMAGO
OASIS
TREND
VERSO

6 letters
DAMASK
FAVOUR
LIMPID
ORANGE
SILICA
SPLINT

7 letters
ABOLISH
APPEASE
ECLIPSE
FUNERAL
ROLLMOP
SUSPEND
UNAIDED
VISIBLE

Turn To Page 173 For Solutions

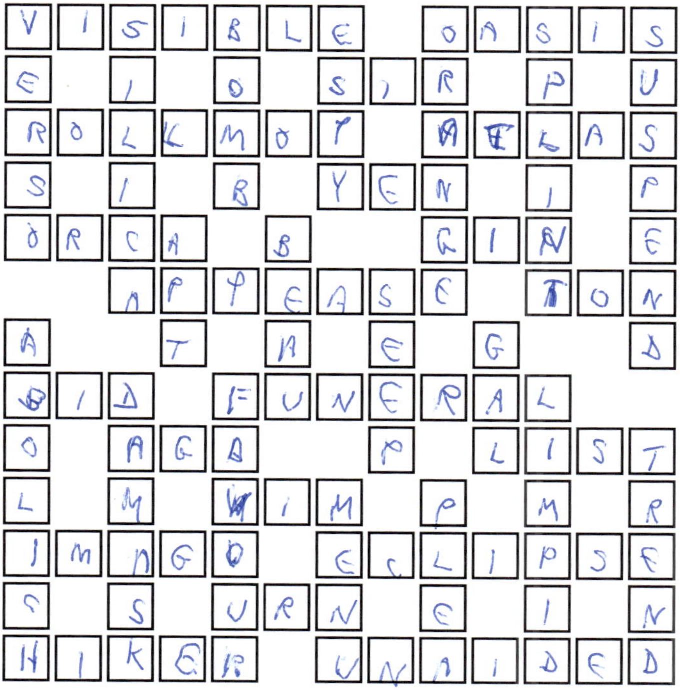

Journey Of A Lifetime

A new holiday adventure beckoned, but for the luxury-loving couple, going back to basics might be a bumpy ride...

Whether it was down to global warming or simply one of the many side effects of growing older, Jan found that she could no longer tolerate holidays abroad during the peak summer months.

She occasionally thought back to trips she'd enjoyed as a young woman, when she'd spent hours lying on a beach in a tiny bikini (unbelievable!), rubbing baby oil into her skin to get a deeper tan (unhinged!).

On recent trips abroad, Jan had sensibly avoided going out into the sun between noon and 4pm, and had used factor 50 suncream at all times.

It had still been too hot to bear, though.

"Can we just avoid going abroad in the summer, do you think?" she asked her husband, Nick, one night as they were having dinner. "I think I've had enough of hot weather."

He smiled at her.

"Are you sure about that? Even when it's freezing cold here, with gale-force winds and torrential rain?"

Jan thought about the unreliable weather they'd often experienced during British summers, comparing it to the bright sunlight and deep, blue skies of foreign countries,

She nodded anyway.

"I just don't think I can handle the forty degree temperatures they get in Mediterranean countries.

"From now on, Europe should be for winter," she added.

Nick ate a forkful of pasta and nodded.

"In that case, what do we do in the summer?"

Despite having lived in the UK their entire lives, Jan and Nick had barely seen any of the country.

They'd been to London, of course, and Edinburgh on a city break, but they'd rarely visited coastal locations and had never ventured to the far north.

There was a lot to choose from, they agreed.

"I just don't think I can handle the forty degree temperatures"

So where should they go on holiday?

Over the next few days, they came up with a handful of possibilities between them.

Blackpool, maybe, to visit the famous Pleasure Beach and the Tower? Or the stunning beaches and coves of Devon and Cornwall? Or perhaps a walking trip in the Lake District? ›

IMAGES: DCT

"I feel guilty we've neglected this country for so long," Nick said.

"There are so many different parts of it that I feel we should see – how are we going to fit it all in?"

Jan came up with a solution of sorts a couple of days later.

"This is a bit random, but why don't we hire a campervan and drive around a few different areas at a time?"

Nick smiled.

"Seriously? Would you be up for that?"

They were at the stage in their life where their holiday accommodation usually involved a stylish hotel or a fancy resort.

This was to be an experience – not just a straightforward holiday

"A campervan might be a bit more cramped than what we're used to..." he added.

"Our first holiday together was in a two-man tent, Nick, and we survived that!" Jan grinned.

"It might do us good to go back to basics."

Once they'd made the decision, the holiday plan took shape.

They scheduled a week in August and decided to head north to the Highlands, booking a decent two-berth campervan to get them started.

It wasn't cheap – a week in Spain would have cost less – but they reasoned that they were paying for more than just accommodation.

This was to be an experience – not just a straightforward holiday.

It was certainly different to what they were used to.

As they drove off in the van on their first day, following a quick tutorial from the man at the rental company ("Make sure everything's packed away before driving, turn off the gas supply at night, and keep your water levels topped up"), the open road stretched in front of them.

"This is what freedom feels like!" Nick said, as he adjusted his sunglasses and popped a Liquorice Allsort into his mouth.

"We can go anywhere we want and do anything we like!"

Jan smiled back.

It did feel good to be together like this, driving somewhere new, with only each other for company.

After all, in their busy lives, how often did they just sit together for hours on end, as they were doing now?

The rain started almost immediately, beginning with a thundery downpour then settling into a constant, mid-level drizzle.

"Welcome to Scotland," Jan muttered.

The van's windscreen wipers kept a steady rhythm as they drove through the downpour.

They felt sure they were surrounded by breathtaking scenery, but it was hard to tell with the reduced visibility.

After a few hours of driving, Nick suggested they stop for lunch.

With no towns or villages in sight, they parked and climbed into the back of the van, planning to heat up a tin of soup to have with some crackers and cheese they'd brought with them.

They fiddled with the gas canister, forgot how to turn on the water supply, and then couldn't work out how to attach the cooking pots to their dinky little handles.

The soup heated up too fast and overflowed on to the tiny cooker, and Nick bumped his head as he jumped up to clear up the mess. And the rain kept falling.

They munched on the dry crackers – they'd forgotten to pack butter – and reminisced about meals from holidays past.

Delicious fresh prawns they'd eaten by the sea in Andalucia... Amazing stuffed pasta in Tuscany... Hot, flavoursome stews in the Dordogne...

Nick took another bite of his cracker and smiled at Jan.

"Still, we always feel like we've overdone it when we come back from foreign trips – this is much healthier!"

The rain eventually stopped, leaving the scenery around them looking fresh and full of colour, and they followed the map to stop at a golden, sandy beach.

As they looked out over the turquoise waters of the Atlantic, the sun suddenly appeared from behind the clouds, turning the sand a sparkling silver.

They got out of the van and wandered down to the water's edge.

"I'm going to go for a swim," Jan announced impulsively.

She swam regularly at her local pool and was in the sea every day whenever they went on beach holidays abroad, but rarely had water look as enticing as this.

The waves rippled at her feet, and the sea was so clear they could see tiny fish flicking about beneath the surface.

She ran back to the van and changed into her swimsuit, then waded confidently into the sea, with Nick staring at her in a mixture of disbelief and admiration.

The cold hit her with a shock, and she screamed aloud in genuine pain.

"Argh! It's freezing!" she yelled. "How can it be this cold? It's summer, for goodness' sake!"

Nick could only laugh, relieved he was still fully dressed, as Jan ran back out of the sea and sprinted for the van.

They made hot chocolate on the gas cooker and wrapped blankets around themselves to get warm.

Jan worried about the possibility of having hypothermia and Nick remarked that it was a concern he'd never heard from her on previous summer holidays.

"Remember when we were lying on that beach on the Costa del Sol, where it was so hot we didn't even have the energy to drag ourselves to the sea?" he said.

"Then when we did finally dive in, the water was so warm it felt like a bath."

Jan sipped her hot chocolate and shook her head in disbelief.

How could two beaches feel so different, not just in temperature but in atmosphere?

That night, after checking into a quaint but basic campsite, Nick heated up a tin of curry, burned some rice and broke a corkscrew trying to open a bottle of wine.

They ate their supper in thoughtful contemplation, thinking about previous holiday meals, then visited the outdoor toilet (a chemical drain in a wooden shed) before settling down for their first night's sleep.

This involved pulling out the seating in the van to create a small double bed (basically a single) and snuggling in together under a light duvet.

It was certainly cosy and Jan thought about all the super-sized hotel beds they had slept in throughout their marriage, when they would lie feet apart from each other with an expanse of mattress between them.

The next morning, she was surprised to wake up feeling fully rested and warm and relaxed.

Nick wasn't quite so enthusiastic and moaned about the bed being too short, meaning his feet had stuck out the bottom of it all night. ›

"That's what you get for being six feet tall," Jan commented, and they laughed and then attempted to make scrambled egg and sausages for breakfast, along with fresh coffee.

They pulled open the side door of the van and stared at the scene before them, with rugged fields disappearing down to the sea, where the sun was just rising on the horizon.

It was mesmerising.

Each day after that followed a simple routine – breakfast in the van, then a long walk with a picnic lunch, before driving on to a new beach or a castle or a hill to climb.

One of the campsites they stayed in was perched on high cliffs above the sea and they parked the van facing the open expanse of the horizon.

They made dinner – a simple stir-fry, with Nick getting more used to the doll-sized pots and pans – and then settled down to read.

Jan was engrossed in a novel set in the frozen wastes of Siberia, which made Scotland feel positively balmy, and Nick had got back into the habit of reading a daily newspaper and doing the crossword.

He'd occasionally ponder clues out loud – "Brokering peace, seven letters...?" – and was genuinely elated when he managed to complete the entire puzzle.

Daylight seemed to last forever, so much so they barely had to use the van's interior lights.

After finishing each chapter of her book, Jan would glance up and look out of the windscreen, always surprised to see the stunning view again, and entranced as she watched the most amazing sunset unfold before her eyes.

The sky changed slowly and beautifully, with dramatic swathes of orange, pink and gold lighting the dusk, as the sun dipped towards the horizon on the sea in a glowing ball of light.

She kept putting her book down to take photos of the sky, keen to capture the moment – and just when she thought she'd caught the perfect shot, she'd look up from her book again and see that the colours and light had changed once more.

As they were getting ready for bed one evening, Jan scrolled through her phone and realised she had taken over 50 photos of the sunset.

They stared at the scene before them, where the sun was rising on the horizon

Nick put down his crossword and stood outside the van door, stretching and yawning.

"It's funny not having a TV, isn't it?" he said with a smile.

"Or a laptop, or WiFi... Remember the huge TV we had in our hotel room in Florida, the one that had about a hundred channels?"

Jan smiled. "Yeah, but we still couldn't find anything worth watching."

Yet here, in the van, their attention had been held for hours by the simple pleasures of a book, a crossword and a jaw-dropping sunset.

They continued driving, clinging to the west coast and keeping their eyes on the sea.

Nick surprised Jan by connecting his phone to the van stereo using Bluetooth.

He then blasted out a playlist he had made of songs they had listened to when they had first started going out together, ›

and the sweet romance of this gesture touched Jan more than she'd expected.

The winding roads unspooled before them as they drove along the coastline, and they spotted eagles in the sky and dolphins leaping from the water.

They bought hot, vinegary fish and chips and ate them sitting on a harbour wall, and toured a whisky distillery, where they bought a sample of the local malt which they sipped each night as they watched the sunset.

"Remember those fancy cocktails we had at the resort in Greece?" Jan said one evening, and they laughed about how tipsy they'd got as they'd danced the night away at the hotel disco.

The place had been so busy and buzzing – totally different to their quiet nights in the van, where it often felt as though they could be the only two people in the world.

One day, they found a small wooden building at the side of the road that contained three basic shower cubicles, built by the local community and operated by dropping a couple of pound coins into a slot.

They both enjoyed a five-minute hot shower, rinsing the sand and salt from their hair, and rubbing their skin dry until it stung.

"Not quite as luxurious as that spa break in Turkey," Nick laughed afterwards, reminding Jan about the whirlpool spa, the sauna and the hot stone massage they'd enjoyed there.

Still, the coin-operated shower felt perfectly adequate in their current surroundings.

All too soon, their week came to an end, and they drove back to the campervan hire location, eating the last of the Liquorice Allsorts on the way, chatting and laughing about all the things they'd seen and done that week.

They left the van behind, got back into their car – it felt so small and low down! – and then drove south towards home.

On the drive back they discussed their trip in detail.

Nick mentioned the cramped living conditions, the awkward cooking facilities, and the lack of basic hygiene and washing space.

Jan talked about the weather, which had ranged from cold to lukewarm to sunny during the week, and the freezing sea water and icy rivers they had paddled in.

The sweet romance of this gesture touched Jan more than she'd expected

They had worn pretty much the same clothes all week, had eaten tinned food most nights, and had given up on things that used to be considered everyday essentials, such as deodorant and mascara.

"So, overall, how would you sum up the trip?" Nick asked as they approached the outskirts of their hometown, familiar sights drawing into view.

Jan looked at him, smiling, and said simply, "Best holiday ever."

Nick grinned in agreement and then went one step further.

"I think we should buy a campervan."

As they laughed, both of them knowing without any doubt that this was going to happen, they looked out of the windscreen at the road ahead, and saw many more happy holidays to come.

By Marie Penman

Brain Boosters

Sudoku

	6	1	7					
7	8							
2				5		6	4	7
4				3	9			
		5	2			9		
			1		4			5
		8		1		3		
		9						6
		7			6		5	1

Fill in each of the blank squares with the numbers 1 to 9, so that each row, each column and each 3x3 cell contains all the numbers from 1 to 9.

Turn To Page 173 For Solutions

Word Wheel

You have ten minutes to find as many words as possible using the letters in the wheel. Each word must be three letters or more and contain the central letter. Use each letter once and no plurals, foreign words or proper nouns are allowed. There is at least one nine-letter word.

New Girls

Whether you're five or twenty-five, a first day is always daunting – yet at the same time full of possibilities

Elspeth looked again at the crumpled piece of paper in her hand. *Staff entrance, side door. Ring the bell and wait.* It had seemed so straightforward when she'd copied down the instructions last night, but she'd rung the bell twice now and no one had come.

While she hovered indecisively, wondering whether she should ring again, a woman swept up and keyed a number into the pad beside the bell. There was a click and a buzz as the door opened.

She glanced at Elspeth.

"Have you forgotten the code?" she asked with a raised eyebrow.

Heat flooded Elspeth's face. She pulled out her piece of paper, but all she saw was the smiley face five-year-old Mia had drawn on it with crayon at breakfast and her eyes filled with tears.

"I'm n . . . not sure."

The woman's phone rang and she snatched it out of her pocket.

"I have to take this. Look, just sign in at reception and . . . ah! Alan." A man had followed them through the main door and she greeted him with relief. "Can you help this woman? She's new. Thanks. Hello?" she said into her phone. "Speaking. Is everything all right?"

He found her name and winced. "Oops. Looks like you just met your new boss"

What code? Elspeth's anxious mind went into tailspin. Code of conduct? Secret code? Dress code?

She opened her mouth to explain she hadn't worked for years, was so nervous she felt sick, that she had just left her young daughter in tears at her new school and that she felt very close to tears herself. Thankfully she said none of those things.

"This is my first day. I'm sorry, I wasn't given any code."

The woman stood aside and let her in.

"Where are you working?"

"Er . . . here." Elspeth was puzzled.

"I mean which department?" she said impatiently. "We have several new starters today."

She glanced at the lift, saw it was ascending and, still talking into her phone, hurried off up the stairs without another glance at Elspeth.

Alan at least seemed friendly.

"Sorry. Traffic was terrible. I should have been here to greet you." He quickly logged into a computer at reception, found her name and winced. "Oops. Looks like you've just met your new boss."

"Seriously?"

"I'm sure her bark's worse than her bite," he said reassuringly.

"Don't you know?"

He shook his head. "She's new, like you. Only started last week. Don't worry, I'm sure you'll be fine. Fourth floor. Look for Ms West's office."

IMAGES: DCT

Or she could just go home now. With a heavy heart, Elspeth took the lift.

She found the office easily enough and since she didn't know when she might get another chance, sneaked a peek at her phone to see if the school had left any messages.

They hadn't, but unfortunately her boss chose that moment to open her office door and did not seem overly impressed by the sight of her new employee loitering outside playing on her phone.

The friendly smiles froze on both women's faces as they suddenly recognised each other.

"Elspeth?"

"Ms West?"

"The other woman flushed pink.

"Call me Sara." She hugged her daughter and told Elspeth, "I owe you an apology. I've been worrying about Lacey all day, but that's no excuse for the way I treated you."

"It's OK," mumbled Elspeth.

Relief filled her when the classroom door opened and Mia ran out giggling

"You're with me? Please come in."

Ms West was professional but distant as they worked their way through the induction paperwork – which included external door codes. There was no chat, no personal questions, no attempt to put Elspeth at ease. She was glad to be passed on to another member of staff to learn her new job role.

****

Later, waiting at the school gates for Mia, Elspeth felt exhausted but relieved to have put her first day behind her.

She desperately hoped that Mia had had a better day than her.

Relief filled her when the classroom doors opened and Mia ran out giggling with another little girl.

"Oh, thank goodness she's made a friend." It was Elspeth's sentiments, but the words came from a woman standing behind her, arms outstretched to welcome Mia's companion. "I've been so worried about her."

"I know what you mean," said Elspeth. "It's Mia's first day. I left her in tears and I've been distracted all day. In fact, I made a total fool of myself at work."

"No, it isn't." The two children wriggled free of their mothers and ran off to play. "We've just moved here. I got a promotion, you see, and so we uprooted the family and relocated.

"But my husband hasn't managed to find a job yet and neither of us realised just how disruptive the move would be for Lacey. It's been incredibly stressful. This is the happiest I've seen her all week."

Elspeth smiled.

"I'm glad she's settled. I'm sure Mia would love to have her round for tea sometime."

"Oh, that would be wonderful," said Sara with a genuine smile.

Her new boss wasn't nearly as intimidating as Elspeth had initially thought; she was simply another working mum under pressure.

"Why don't you come too?" she added impulsively.

Sara positively beamed.

"Thanks. I'd like that. I know we started off on the wrong foot, but it would be great if we new girls could stick together from now on."

By Jacqui Cooper

Brain Boosters

Codeword

Each letter of the alphabet has been replaced by a number. The numbers for the first name of a celebrity are given. Work out which number represents which letter to reveal at which upmarket Mayfair restaurant Gordon Ramsay trained under Albert Roux.

A B C D E F G H I J K L M N O P Q R S T U V W X Y Z

1	2	3	4	5	6	7	8	9	10	11	12	13
									R			

14	15	16	17	18	19	20	21	22	23	24	25	26
G	O						N			D		

19	16		14	6	4	10	15	5	12	16
			G			R	O			

Turn To Page 173 For Solutions

Pumpkins

For childhood friends, village life brought a chance to put down new roots together…

Back in the early nineties it was the custom to go trick-or-treating around the neighbours' houses in our small village.

Most of the villagers were good sports. Even if they didn't welcome the idea of a rabble of unruly children turning up on their doorsteps as soon as dusk fell, they didn't turn us away empty-handed.

Debs and I were always the ringleaders. Our mums were best friends and so were we.

Of the two of us, I was the quiet one. I was an only child, but Debs was much more extrovert.

She was one of three. Her sister, Karen, was five years older than us and her brother, Graham, just two years older.

Karen was way above trick-or-treating, she'd just discovered boys, but Graham sometimes came with us.

"To make sure you don't cause too much mischief," he'd say, laughing good-naturedly as he pulled on his denim jacket and grabbed a torch.

"We wouldn't dream of it, would we?" Debs would roll her eyes and I'd widen mine.

I secretly liked it when Graham came with us. He was nice. He didn't speak down to me like some of the other older lads in the village, and we did have fun on those nighttime forays, creeping along the dark streets that smelled of bonfire smoke and wood fire.

Most of the villagers played along with trick-or-treat. Even Eleanor Knotts at number 33, who was very old and had a black cat which was enough to earn her the title of a witch, often donned a pointy black hat and hid behind her gate pillars so she could jump out at us when we called.

However, she always came up with treats in the end, a handful of dolly mixtures or a jar of boiled sweets from the corner shop.

Eleanor Knotts was what my mother described as a kind old soul.

The only person who didn't welcome us was Old Man Parr who lived alone in the gatehouse on the very outskirts of the village.

Old Man Parr had a scrubby grey beard, cross eyes and a face wrinkled into a permanent frown.

"I reckon he's a money launderer," our dad was fond of saying

He also had a shiny, red sports car, which our dad said he'd probably got from criminal activities. This was because – as far as anyone could tell – Old Man Parr didn't work, and although he looked pretty old to Debs and I, he didn't really look old enough to retire.

"I reckon he's a money launderer," our dad was fond of saying every time we passed the car.

›

"I'm sure he isn't," Mum would say peaceably.

"He's probably got more money than most because he doesn't have any kids or a wife to support."

Whereupon Dad would laugh and say, "You might have a point there, love."

Anyway, the fact that Old Man Parr might be a criminal working on the dark side was enough to make him the perfect target for trick-or-treating for anyone who was brave enough, and it was Debs who suggested we try him one Hallowe'en when we were about 11.

"I'm not sure, Debs. I don't think he'll give us anything."

"Then we'll have to trick him, won't we?

"We can run faster than him, so he won't be able to catch us," she added.

"Are you sure? It's not like he's really old," I said.

"He's probably only about forty-one or something."

"That's old enough to be really slow. Are you chicken, Tracey Baker?" she taunted. "Or are you coming with me?"

"Of course I'm coming."

I was secretly terrified but there was no way I'd let her go alone.

We left him till last which was, with hindsight, a mistake, because we had lots to carry by then.

We were weighed down with sweets and chocolate from the night's haul by the time we got to the gatehouse.

I was half hoping he'd be out, but his car was there, and a single lit window shone out into the night.

We went up the front path and banged on the door.

"Trick or treat?" we yelled in unison.

There was silence.

The curtain in the lit window didn't so much as twitch.

I shrugged. "Well, we tried, didn't we?"

"I think we should try again," Debs said mutinously.

"Maybe he's deaf. Everyone else at least comes to the door."

"Clear off," came a muffled reply from somewhere inside. "Or you'll be sorry"

This time she opened the letterbox and yelled through.

"Trick or treat!"

"Clear off," came a muffled reply from somewhere inside. "Or you'll be sorry."

Debs looked outraged.

"That not how it works," she hissed, kicking the door.

"Don't. We don't want to rile him too much," I said. "Let's just go."

"Not without playing a trick."

She glanced around the dark front garden, but there wasn't so much as a flowerpot we could topple over.

"I know," she said, as I tried to pull her out of the gate.

"We can let his tyres down."

"Debs, no," I protested, but it was too late.

She was already crouched by the sports car, unscrewing a dust cap.

"Help me, Tracey."

She'd just moved to a second tyre when the door of the house opened to reveal an oblong of light and a furious Old Man Parr who'd clearly spotted us.

We did get away. Debs was right, we could run faster than him, but it was a close thing and I dropped my bag of treats in my haste so we lost all of them.

The worst thing was that my school scarf was in that bag, too, and it had my name sewn into the seam, so Old Man Parr knew exactly where to come to find us.

Or at least, he knew where to find me.

****

Across the years, the story of that night grew larger in the retelling. The skies were darker, the taunting louder, the escape riskier.

Old Man Parr had threatened to beat us within an inch of our lives. He'd also become a faster runner.

The punishment our parents meted out grew bigger in the retelling, too.

Debs and I were grounded for a month, instead of just a few days.

Graham was grounded for not stopping us – even though he hadn't even been there.

The only truth that survived intact was that it was our last trick-or-treat.

We finished on a high – or a low, depending on your perspective.

I'm not sure what happened to Old Man Parr, but he didn't stay in the village.

My memories of him moving are hazy, as are Graham's and Debs', but by then we had other things to think about.

Graham and I had become an item. He asked me out when I was 17 and he was 19.

Graham was doing an apprenticeship at the engineering factory and I was working at the local pig farm as a bookkeeper.

When Graham proposed on my 18th birthday, I was over the moon, and we began saving to get married.

Debs had gone away to college. She always was the clever one although, as it happened, she had to drop out in her second year because she got pregnant.

She and Danny had the baby and a quiet wedding with just a few guests, throwing confetti and cheering as they came out of the registry office.

I was both sad and happy for her. We'd always had this fantasy we'd have our kids around the same age and they'd grow up together and become best friends and maybe one day, even do trick-or-treat together, but Graham and I weren't ready to become parents back then.

"I want our kids to have the things we didn't have," Graham said.

"And I want us to have a big wedding where you get to go in a horse and carriage to the church."

We got our big wedding in our mid 20s but we didn't get the babies. Not even one baby came along.

Not that we didn't have kids in our life. Debs' children were a joy – she had three by then, and being Aunt and Uncle to them was fun and tiring and lovely.

It turned out I was the one with the fertility issues. We spent a fortune on IVF, but no go and, in the end, I said to Graham, "I won't blame you if you want to find someone you can have a family with. I know how much family means to you."

We'd always had this fantasy we'd have our kids around the same age

"No way," Graham said, cupping my face in his and looking into my eyes.

"I'm here for the duration, Tracey. I've always loved you, and I always will."

****

When we were in our mid 30s, Graham and I packed in our jobs and bought a smallholding, a parcel of land just a stone's throw from the gatehouse where › the infamous Old Man Parr once lived.

Owning a smallholding was another dream, and this was one we could achieve.

These days, Graham grows organic vegetables and sells them to the farm shop – it's now an artisan farm shop, and the farm's a petting farm.

I help. I also foster dogs and cats for a local rescue centre.

There's plenty of room and it goes a long way towards satisfying my nurturing instincts.

This year we grew pumpkins for Hallowe'en.

Debs suggested we have a 'Pick Your Own Pumpkin' day and it's been a huge success.

"Oh, Trace. I'm sorry." She looks stricken. "I didn't mean to upset..."

"You haven't," I reassure her instantly. "This is mad, and you're not going to believe it, but..." I cup my tummy and her eyes widen as she follows my gaze.

"You're kidding. You're not...?"

"Yep. At the grand old age of thirty-nine, I'm finally pregnant.

"We didn't want to jinx it or I'd have told you before but we had the twelve week scan yesterday and it's official. We're expecting..." I glance around us smiling. "A little pumpkin of our own..."

"Oh, my God, that's amazing."

As she hugs me, I blink back tears. My lovely friend and sister-in-law. I can't remember a time without her.

Owning a smallholding was another dream, one we could achieve

Debs became a primary school teacher in the end, and she encouraged all her pupils to bring their parents to our pumpkin field.

The smallholding has echoed with the excited shouts of children all day.

Debs and I are outside now, standing at the five-bar gate looking across the field at the few pumpkins left unpicked.

They look like tiny golden globes beneath a sunset-streaked sky.

"Do you remember Old Man Parr?" Debs asks me with a mock shudder.

"I still have nightmares about him catching us," I said. "We thought he was old, didn't we, and we're the same age now. Well, Graham is..."

She giggled. "I know. I do feel a bit guilty sometimes. That car was his pride and joy but he did hate kids, didn't he?"

"Or maybe he just couldn't have any," I say reflectively. "So he didn't understand them."

"A couple of days ago she'd told me that Rosie, her eldest, was expecting and I'd been so tempted to tell her we were, too, but I'm glad we waited.

I notice Graham is heading down a line of pumpkins towards us.

He's seen his sister's reaction, so can guess our conversation.

"Maybe one day in the future our child and your grandchild can go trick-or-treating together," I say as Graham reaches us.

"Won't that be a thing?"

'Oh, yes." Debs' eyes dance with expectation. "We'll have to go with them. Parents do these days. Make sure they stay out of mischief."

"That's definitely something to look forward to," Graham agrees, and his smile matches the warmth of the sunset as he leans in to hug us both close.

By Della Galton

Brain Boosters

Kriss Kross

Try to fit all of the listed words back into the grid.

4 letters
COVE
OAST
THAT
TIRE

5 letters
BASIC
NIECE
STOAT
STOOL

6 letters
ADVERT
BESIDE
MALLET
SURFER
TOUCHY
UNLESS

7 letters
ELASTIC
RETRIAL
SHOWERY
SUNBEAM

8 letters
BIGAMOUS
ESCALOPE
GRANDSON
OBEDIENT

13 letters
DISAPPEARANCE
NEIGHBOURHOOD

Turn To Page 173 For Solutions

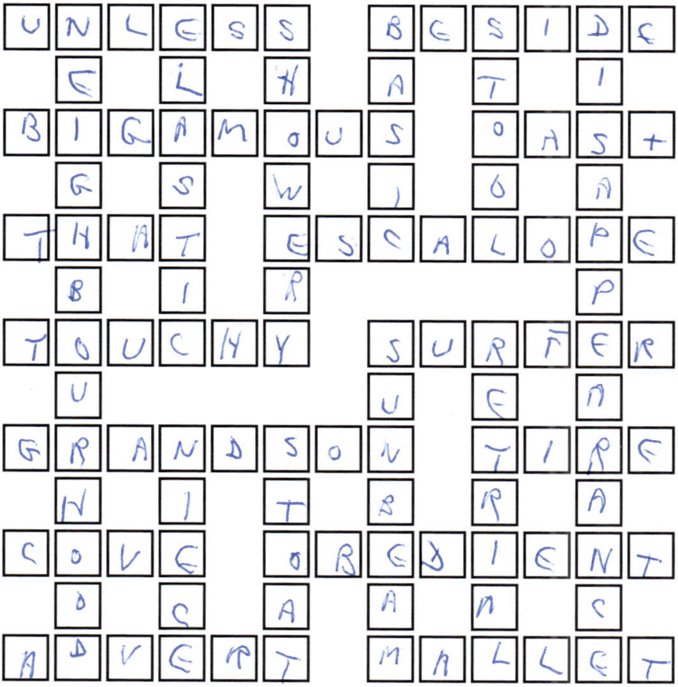

Out Of A Dark Place

Taylor's joy and enthusiasm for Hallowe'en were irresistible – to everyone except Miles, it seemed . . .

Taylor put the freshly baked pumpkin on the kitchen table and stared at her partner, Miles. "Gee, you Brits sure don't know how to have fun!"

"It's not that," Miles said, quietly. "It's just that, unless you're at primary school, Hallowe'en doesn't mean much to us here in the UK. And you know how I feel about the actual day . . ."

Taylor sighed as she tried to slice off the top of the still-warm pumpkin. She knew what Miles meant, but wouldn't go there. It upset him too much – and besides, he already felt pretty negative about her Hallowe'en plans.

Miles had frowned as she'd searched for a plastic bucket to collect the treats she expected to receive.

"Why not?"

"Because . . . well, because it's not an adult thing to do here unless you're accompanying kids, but as we haven't any children of our own . . ." He looked wistful for a moment. "People will think it's weird if we knock on their door and ask for treats without little ones in tow."

Taylor thought for a moment.

"Can't I go hang with a family?"

A look of actual horror crossed Miles' dark features.

Last year hadn't been great, Taylor conceded. She wanted to change it up

Taylor sighed, gliding around the kitchen in her long black dress with lace sleeves that Miles always liked her in, as she concentrated on her plans for the weekend ahead.

Back in the States, she'd loved the special holiday. Mom would decorate the house with jack-o'-lanterns, grown-ups and kids alike would dress up and there were so many parties, she couldn't choose which to go to.

But here in the UK, which she loved for the rest of the year, Hallowe'en was a disconcertingly muted affair.

Take last year . . .

"You can't go trick-or-treating, Taylor," "No! That would be even odder. Sorry, Taylor – please can you just accept that here in the UK, we just do things differently for Hallowe'en?"

Yes – last year hadn't been great, Taylor conceded. And that's why she wanted to change it up this year. Even if Miles had his own reasons for not celebrating Hallowe'en.

****

Miles had finally finished getting through to all Taylor's friends. How he'd managed it without her finding out, he didn't know. The woman had a sixth sense, and then some.

IMAGES: DCT

He limped across their bedroom, wondering how he'd be able to keep the details secret until Friday. Taylor had a way of discovering everything. He'd never been able to surprise her.

He gazed out of the window onto the road below just as a motorbike roared by. He flinched. Didn't the rider realise how dangerous bikes could be?

He shrugged, feeling hypocritical. Had he worried when he'd been a rider?

No, he'd loved speeding along coastal roads with the wind in his face, changing lanes on the motorways or even whizzing along winding country lanes. But all that stopped abruptly three years ago when he'd had his accident.

He shuddered, his memories a sea of screams, skidding tyres on the frosty road, blue lights blinking, unfamiliar hands touching, lifting him . . .

The only good to come out of it had been meeting Taylor. In fact he was certain that if he hadn't crashed, he'd never have met the willowy brunette. As his mum had always told him, "Something good always comes from something bad."

Although he hadn't known at the time, Taylor had cared for him from the moment he'd been admitted to hospital. It was over a week before he came out of his coma and met the young medic from Connecticut who had a special transitional role at the hospital, nursing and nurturing those in her care.

"Bike accident, hey?" she'd asked, checking his vital signs.

He'd nodded, but the movement had sent shockwaves through him.

"Can you guess how many guys I see in here who've gotten injuries from falling from their bikes? You'd never catch me on one," she'd declared firmly.

Miles had lain in bed, monitors bleeping, tubes coming out of places he didn't even know he had. Unable to move, he doubted he'd ever ride his bike again.

He'd been passionate about his motorbike but after being so badly injured, the crash had been a real wake-up call. At only thirty, there was so much life he still wanted to live.

Taylor had cared for him from the moment he'd been admitted

As each day passed with this beautiful woman nursing him, teasing him when he was down, explaining gently how his life had changed and helping him move on, he knew he wanted to share every moment with her – if she'd have him.

Now as he pushed the memories away, he tried to concentrate on his plans for the weekend. Taylor would love it!

****

Where was Miles? Taylor wondered. Lately, he kept disappearing. Had he found someone else?

She bit her lip. She'd never loved anyone as she loved him, but they were so very different.

She was a typical American who loved everything to do with her culture – Independence Day, Thanksgiving, Labor Day and, of course, Hallowe'en.

Miles was a typical Brit. He was reserved, painfully polite and obsessed with the weather. She loved him, but couldn't help noticing the differences between them. And now he was more reserved than ever.

Sometimes she'd suggest brightly, "Let's go to the coast, try out the zip wire on the beach or jump aboard a jet ski."

Yet he never wanted to. He liked to stay home. Since leaving hospital, he'd become totally risk-averse.

She'd encourage him to go out, meet people, to no avail.

"It's hard walking with my leg. And I don't like facing people like this," he'd say, pointing to the scars on his face.

She'd often tell him how attractive she felt they made him.

"I think your scars are sexy. They make you look rugged. And besides, they're a reminder of how we met."

"You'd find a silver lining in a disaster." He'd shrug his wide shoulders and smile.

As Taylor set to work, moving through the hospital until she reached the ward she was assigned to today, she thought it wasn't just her nationality that made her positive; her work did, too. Caring for critically ill patients had been as natural for her as dressing up for Hallowe'en.

****

Miles limped around the room, draping wispy strands over doors to look like spiders' webs, lighting candles and putting pumpkins around the fireplace. Even Taylor would be impressed. He smiled.

The guests were arriving half an hour before she came home. Miles couldn't wait to surprise her. She was a wonderful woman who'd looked after him and all her other patients so well. He wanted to show her how much he cared.

She was naturally gregarious and sociable. He knew she missed spending time with friends, but lived like a recluse for his sake. But lately he'd sensed a change – since meeting Adam at the hospital, when he collected Taylor, one afternoon, from the children's ward.

"What's your name?" the pale little boy with shadows under his eyes asked as he sat with his mum in the corridor.

Miles had told him.

"And what's wrong with your face?"

"Adam!" his mum scolded.

"No, it's all right," Miles had replied, gently explaining his bike accident.

"My face had an argument with the road, but the road won."

The little boy laughed and said, "I'm here for my poorly tummy. But the doctors will make me better."

As Miles chatted to Adam and his family, peace settled over him. These people didn't view him any differently, so why should he worry?

Slowly, over time, he began to feel ready to mix again. To spend time with friends. And what better way than at a Hallowe'en party?

****

"Taylor will love this!" Josh exclaimed when Miles opened the door. "Your apartment looks great!"

Josh, dressed as Dracula with an impressive set of fangs, stepped into the hall and looked around appreciatively.

"I hope so," Miles said. "I've worked all day while she was at the hospital."

"You won't be able to surprise her," warned Josh's brother, Lewis, who was a pirate. "She always finds out somehow."

Miles laughed.

"Well, maybe this time I'll succeed. She thinks I'm not really into Hallowe'en, so she won't be expecting anything."

"You've done her proud," said Violet, in a long, ragged dress and looking positively ghostly with her face painted white. "This will be a Hallowe'en party she'll always remember."

"She's helped so many of us. It's only right that I give her something back." Miles smiled.

"Good to see you mixing with people again, Miles," Josh said, hovering by the long table where the buffet was laid out.

Miles smiled, tightly.

"It's hard, but I think I'm ready to face the world again."

"No doubt that's Taylor's influence."

He nodded as more of her friends arrived. Now all he had to do was get everyone into position, dim the lights and wait for Taylor to come home.

****

The shift had been difficult. Taylor had nursed Nancy, a young girl who'd fallen off her horse, for several days but she'd made a miraculous recovery. All the team were talking about it.

Taylor was pleased, of course, but she'd miss Nancy. Over the last few days she'd become attached to the young girl.

Tomorrow she'd be moved on to a regular ward and their paths would probably never cross again.

"Our job is all about goodbyes, one way or another," her colleague said.

"Sure, but it don't get any easier."

She was still thinking about Nancy when she arrived home. Preoccupied, she slid her key in the door, surprised the apartment was in darkness. She didn't have long to get ready for Hallowe'en, she thought, turning on the light.

"Surprise!" Miles shouted.

Taylor jumped, then laughed in delight as she gazed around the decorated hall.

"Wow! You sure done me proud. The apartment looks great!"

"Yes –" he reached for the door handle – "and there's something else."

He pushed open the door. Taylor covered her mouth with her hands, clearly shocked to see all her old friends.

"It's party time!" he laughed.

"Oh Miles, how fantastic," Taylor said, hugging friends she hadn't seen for ages.

"As good as you had in the States?"

"Better! I know how hard this must be for you. Yet you did it for me."

Miles pulled her close and kissed her.

"Of course. Happy Hallowe'en, darling. You've helped us all so much. I wanted to give you something back."

****

Later, Miles and Taylor sat outside under the stars.

"Did you enjoy the party?" he asked.

"Oh yes! It's why I love Hallowe'en – the chance to connect with people I've known for, well, centuries. But I know it reminds you of the day of your accident."

"It was my fault. If I hadn't been speeding to a party, I wouldn't have crashed." Miles pulled her close.

"I know how hard this must be for you. Yet you did it for me"

"And you wouldn't have met me."

"Mmm. And now I get to spend forever with you."

"It's not so bad being this side, is it?"

"No, and I get to do fun things like walk through walls, listen in on people's conversations, and move around quicker than I ever could on my bike.

"But it's all down to you. You helped so many to move on. Like you did me, the day I came out of my coma."

"You were too injured to go back so I brought you here. And now you get to stay. Forever."

"Of course I miss my old life, but I love being with you." He smiled.

"And perhaps, now, you even love Hallowe'en!"

"You know, my love, I think I do."

By Tess Niland Kimber

Brain Boosters

Sudoku

					2			8
	2	5		7		4		
	3			1			9	
1								6
	9		4			7	3	
4		3		8				
5		2	1				8	
				9		5	6	
		9	3		8			

Fill in each of the blank squares with the numbers 1 to 9, so that each row, each column and each 3x3 cell contains all the numbers from 1 to 9.

Turn To Page 173 For Solutions

Word Wheel

You have ten minutes to find as many words as possible using the letters in the wheel. Each word must be three letters or more and contain the central letter. Use each letter once and no plurals, foreign words or porper nouns are allowed. There is at least one nine-letter word.

No-Vember

With a seasonal sermon to write, the stumped Reverend Jerry needed some divine inspiration – and quickly . . .

Reverend Jerry Grande was trying, and failing, to write his sermon for the final Sunday of November. Usually once he made himself start, the words flowed, but he was stumped.

Remembrance Sunday was easy, topic-wise. He'd suggested that, along with remembering sacrifices of the past, his congregation didn't forget those people who were part of their present.

"Don't wait until someone is lost to you before you remember them in your hearts, prayers and actions," he'd preached. Something like that anyway.

A few mentioned their joy at getting a letter or call in response. Jerry had been gratified his words had such a positive response, and hoped all those who acted on them would experience as much pleasure as the beneficiaries of their thoughtful gestures.

The week before had been even easier in terms of sermon writing. There had been All Saints' Day and Bonfire Night to use as themes. Reverend Grande had spoken about the variety of different saints who'd done lots of different things to earn their canonisation.

Jerry had put a lot of words onto paper – and crossed them all out

He didn't keep the text of old sermons, as the temptation to reuse them might be too great when he was particularly busy. It would be embarrassing if people remembered them – perhaps even worse if it was clear they didn't.

The remembrance sermon was a success, apparently. He'd noticed several people who didn't usually have much company received visits or invitations from neighbours, and several members of his congregation visited relatives they'd not seen recently.

Mary Milligan reported the post office had experienced higher sales of letter-writing stationery, postcards and stamps.

Some of her customers mentioned they were writing to old friends or family members they'd not been in contact with for ages.

"And we, too, are all different and do good in various ways. We have our own methods of bringing light and warmth into the world."

Although it wasn't something he'd consciously intended, he'd been very pleased several members of the congregation remembered his liking for cake and decided to bring him one.

The ginger cake made by Sue North was wonderfully warming. When he said so it was clear she'd not made the connection between his words and her action, but that didn't mean his sermon hadn't been effective.

By early Friday morning, Jerry had put a lot of words onto paper – and crossed them all out. He didn't understand why they didn't satisfy him. They were full of Christian virtues such as caring for your ›

IMAGE: DCT

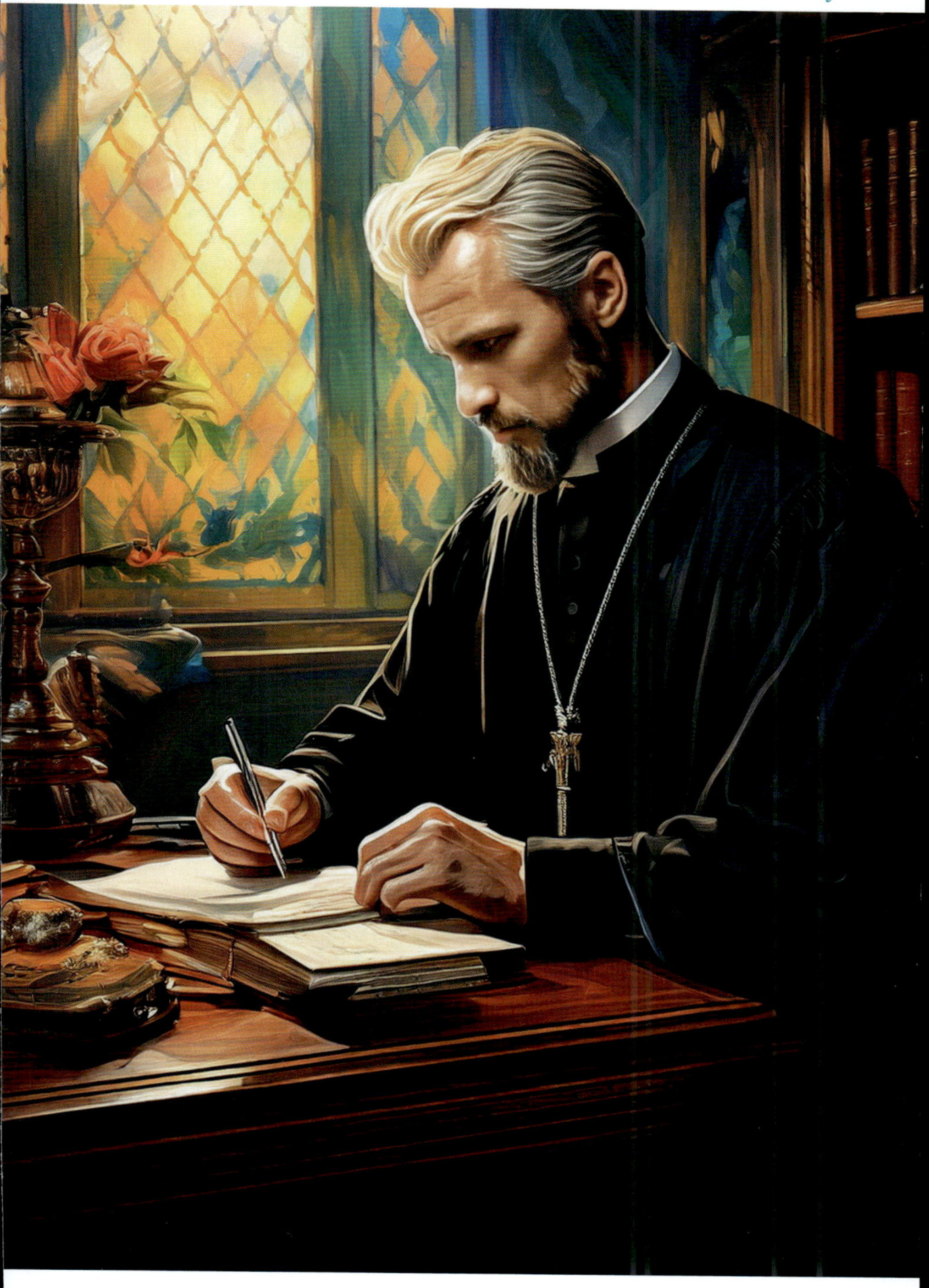

neighbours in the cold, dark days ahead, not forgetting those most disadvantaged, and not being persuaded by beguiling advertisements to forget the true meaning of Christmas.

There was no obvious theme to his thoughts, and no bible story to tie them to; perhaps that was the trouble?

Then it struck him that there was a subliminal connection. Thomas Hood's poem *No!* which was all about the good things from other times of the year which were lacking in November.

That was Jerry's trouble, his thoughts were all negative. No doubt some clergy got good results from playing on people's guilt or promising fire and brimstone – certainly such things had been popular in the past, but they weren't Jerry's style.

He wanted people to leave his services uplifted, secure in God's love and wanting to do what was right because it appealed to their inherent good nature, not because they were scared into it.

The sound of someone singing a few lines from *What a Wonderful World* outside the vicarage window made him look up. It was his nephew, Mike, arriving a little early for a planned visit.

He had a vaguely familiar multicoloured scarf around his neck, almost matching bobble hat on his head, and was juggling more than his usual amount of luggage. There was nothing of the, "No warmth, no cheerfulness, no healthful ease", about him!

Of course, Jerry was hugely biased in his favour, and had been since his dear sister had joyfully announced her pregnancy.

"No traffic on the A27 for once, and a clear run from Fareham down to Little Mallow, so I'm early. Hope that's OK?" Mike said after greeting his uncle with a hug.

"That's no problem at all," Jerry assured him. "Interesting scarf."

"I won it in the Christmas raffle last year," Mike reminded him. "My punishment for contributing to your running away to Barbados fund."

"All proceeds went to the church roof appeal, as well you know."

"So says every vicar everywhere!"

Jerry, used to such teasing, returned the conversation to the scarf. "I didn't realise you actually liked that thing."

No doubt some clergy got good results from playing on people's guilt

"It's obviously hand-made, so I didn't want it to be the last thing to go."

"And now you're wearing it here so whoever made it will see how much you appreciate it."

"I blame you, Uncle. You're a terrible influence on my street cred and bad-boy reputation." Mike indicated Jerry's pile of discarded attempts at a satisfactory sermon. "What's the problem?"

"November!"

"Really? I've always liked the month. I suppose because it's my birthday," Mike said.

"I'm thankful to it for bringing me you, but I don't enjoy it."

He quoted what he could recall of the poem. "No sun, no moon. No dusk, no dawn, no proper time of day. A bit I can't remember then: No shade, no shine, no butterflies, no bees. No fruits, no flowers, no leaves, November!"

Mike grinned.

"You've not read it lately, have you?"

"I take that to mean I didn't get

the words quite right. Considering I've probably not seen them since I was at school, I don't think I did too badly."

"You didn't," Mike agreed. "Personally, I like the poem. There's a nice rhythm to it and beautiful images."

"The rhythm yes, but images? Isn't it the opposite?" Jerry asked.

"In the bit you quoted, but you've forgotten a lot. I'm surprised, as it mentions not only a church but a view of heaven."

"It does?"

"No sky, no earthly view. No distance looking blue. No road, no street, no t'other side the way. No end to any row. No indications where the crescents go. No top to any steeple."

"I confess I'm not quite with you. The steeple is from a church, of course, but images and heaven, where are they?"

"Lost in the mist! That's what the poet is saying – the world is the same, even if we can't see it properly."

"Yes, perhaps that's right." Although what Mike had said made sense, it seemed an odd conversation for them to be having. Mike was far more likely to discuss the plot of a TV murder series than the meaning of classic poetry.

"From what I recall, paying attention wasn't your strongest point at school. I'm impressed you can remember what your teacher said back then."

"Ah! Not my teacher back then, but your teacher much more recently."

"Mine?" As Mike didn't share the reverend's religious conviction, he most likely meant a living person.

"Oh! Miss Jenkins?" The young, infant schoolteacher had a tumble of richly coloured curls and, except on the most solemn occasions, gave the impression she would break into laughter any moment.

She was just the kind of person Jerry would like to see his nephew married to, especially if he got to conduct the service and they were to make their home nearby. Mike visited quite often, but it would be nice to see him even more frequently.

"Uncle Jerry!"

"Oh, sorry. I was . . ."

"Don't say miles away. You were in the church, weren't you? Either christening my kids or giving the sermon I've somehow inspired you to write."

"Guilty – although I'd only got as far as, 'Who gives this woman to be married to this man?'"

"You're still a long way ahead of me."

"Have you had any encouragement in that direction?"

"Not yet, but no discouragement either. I'm taking that as a good sign. She seems nice. Too nice not to give me a hint if she wasn't interested."

"Yes, I think so. Do you fancy a walk to show off that scarf?" Jerry asked.

"If it involves turning right out of the vicarage gate, I do."

As he and Mike began their stroll Mike said, "Looks like it's bin day."

"Thanks for reminding me. The Williamses are on holiday."

Jerry changed direction.

"I'm sure this all makes perfect sense to you."

"The Williamses usually put the wheelie bin out for their neighbour. He's in a wheelchair so it's awkward for him."

After placing the bin ready for collection, Jerry and Mike walked in a loop which just happened to take them past the teacher's home.

They met Bert Grahame wheeling his barrow back from the allotments.

"Good morning," Jerry said. "How are you?"

"Can't complain."

Jerry saw Mike trying to suppress ›

a smile and hoped his own face was doing a better job of hiding the fact he knew Old Bert was more than capable of complaining about his health, the weather, greenfly or almost anything else.

Bert put down the barrow, rubbed his back and grimaced. "At my age . . ."

"Oh!"

"Everything OK, Uncle?"

"Yes, yes. Perfectly fine."

He'd seen Miss Jenkins heading towards them, but that wasn't the reason for his surprised reaction.

Mike pulled off his colourful hat and attempted to stuff it into his jacket pocket, while tucking as much of the scarf out of sight as possible.

Miss Jenkins, a laugh dancing in her eyes, greeted everyone and mentioned how cold it was.

wind was bitterly cold, and it was just about coffee time, Miss Jenkins had never previously invited the reverend into her home.

As far as he knew she'd not offered Old Bert a warming drink and snack before, either.

He was sure she would do so, if she ever thought they were in need, but as both of them lived just a few hundred yards away and neither looked at all malnourished, no particular need was apparent.

Perhaps she was hoping for one of the marvellous-looking parsnips in Bert's wheelbarrow but, as Bert was always generous with surplus vegetables, and was covered with the medium in which he grew them, that seemed unlikely to be her main motivation.

"I've been struggling with my sermon, and the right topic has just come to me"

"Would you all like to come in for a coffee? It's only instant, but I've got some shortbread to go with it."

Mike and Bert Grahame accepted enthusiastically. Jerry declined.

"I've been struggling with my sermon, and the right topic has just come to me."

"Divine inspiration?" Mike asked.

"Not precisely. All three of you have shown me something."

Jerry refused to say more other than to suggest they attend church on Sunday to find out. Mike he knew would be there in any case, if he were still staying with Jerry.

Bert and Miss Jenkins, despite living within walking distance of St Symeon's, were far less regular attendees, but Jerry had a feeling that at least one of them would be there next Sunday.

Although it was perfectly true that the

Mike might not think Miss Jenkins was offering him any encouragement, but Jerry had other ideas.

And, of course, he had the idea for his sermon. That our blessings can be about the absence of something not just its presence.

No pain or sickness is as much a reason to be thankful as a recovery from illness. No pressing money concerns as worthy of celebration as a cash windfall.

Nothing interesting to report far better than bad news to pass on.

Looked at in the right light, the lack of many things could be considered positive.

Even missing out on a piece of shortbread now might, just possibly, be compensated by a slice of wedding cake in the future.

By Patsy Collins

Brain Boosters

Kriss Kross

Try to fit all of the listed words back into the grid.

4 letters
BAIL
GIRL
KETO
RAIL

5 letters
BODGE
HALVA
LATCH
SABLE

6 letters
ALPINE
BASQUE
MAYFLY
SCENIC
SERAPH
SPHERE

7 letters
ACCLAIM
CATHODE
NOISOME
PARSLEY

8 letters
CATHOLIC
OPERETTA
TRAMLINE
UNLISTED

13 letters
CONTEMPLATIVE
UNINTENTIONAL

Turn To Page 173 For Solutions

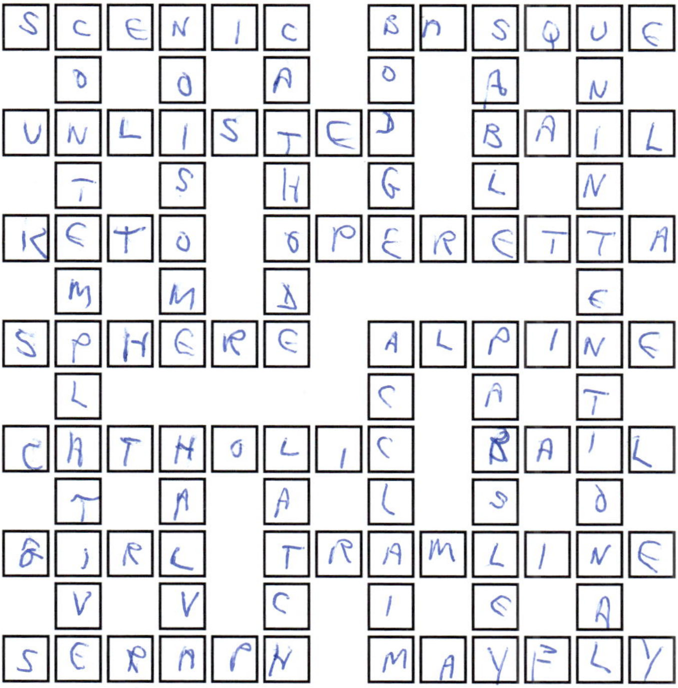

Christmas Chaos

An unexpected festive guest sets the cat among the decorations, but could Katie recover her holiday cheer?

My phone went. It was Simon, calling from work.

"Tom has just rung," he said. "Their plans to go to Lisa's friends for Christmas are off, so I said they could come to us instead. Is that OK with you, Katie?"

"Of course, great!'

"They'll be here tomorrow lunchtime."

He chatted on, but I wasn't listening – just panicking, big-time. Tomorrow was Christmas Eve and Simon's son and daughter-in-law were coming to stay.

I'd been a bit down after hearing that my own son, Adam, was going to his girlfriend's for the holiday.

So, why wasn't I over the moon at this news?

Because, in my mind, I had sort of cancelled Christmas this year. As well as working at the art gallery, I'd been busy painting pictures. Mind you, I did buy a turkey, now sitting in the freezer, so I do get a few brownie points.

"But Simon, the place is a tip."

"Don't worry, I can warn them."

"Warn them? Is it that bad?"

Simon laughed and said he had to go.

Typical of Simon to find this funny, yet his sense of humour was what I'd loved about him from the start. We first met at the gallery and, being widower and divorcée, clicked immediately.

Corny, but true.

I glanced around the lounge. Books, general clutter, chaos and, except for a few cards, nothing festive whatsoever. Long-suffering Bertie, our fluffy Persian, was curled up on a pile of magazines.

However, this muddle suited me. Cosy, I called it. Simon hadn't helped. Proud of my modest success as an artist, he had hung up far too many of my pictures since I moved in with him a year ago.

My use of vivid colour, shouting loudly and merrily from the walls, added to the fray. I made myself a coffee, thinking hard. It would be great to see Tom and Lisa again; they lived miles away and I'd only met them once, yet I felt uneasy.

Lisa: a self-assured accountant. Me: your clichéd scruffy, artistic type

Tom was lovely, but I'd not hit it off a hundred per cent with his wife. She'd been friendly enough, but we were complete opposites.

Lisa: a self-assured accountant with stunning clothes, the kind of lustrous hair you only see in adverts and a minimalist, spotless house. Me: your clichéd scruffy, artistic type with home-cut hair and ›

IMAGE: DCT

topsy-turvy habits.

Bertie sat up, yawning, and I tickled his ears. Was Lisa into cats, I wondered, and what about the smell of oil paint and my disastrous cooking? Will they expect to be taken on a hearty walk after lunch on the big day?

I needed to get festive. I was a bit negative about it last year, too. I had an urgent deadline for a picture, so Simon and Adam had happily scoffed bacon sandwiches and watched *Morecombe and Wise* while I worked.

"Bertie, let's go!" I cried, grabbing a pile of books.

The cat yawned again, but I moved, shoving books into wardrobes and cramming bits and bobs into cupboards and drawers.

After staggering to my studio with another load, I rooted out Mum's old Christmas decorations box and draped everything tinselly and glittery, transforming the room into a real Santa's grotto.

An hour later I took stock. You couldn't exactly call it minimalist with all the Christmas paraphernalia around, but there were now armchairs you could sit on and patches of carpet exposed to the light of day.

"Wow! Very festive!" Simon said, when he came home. "Where have you put everything?"

"Is it OK? Their room still has to be done –"

"Katie," he interrupted. "I'm sorry, but we're really short-staffed for tomorrow's party. So I volunteered."

I frowned. Simon ran a children's charity and already put in many hours.

"But you're supposed to finish at lunchtime!"

"I'll be home late afternoon, in time to hang up my stocking," he laughed, but I just glared.

"Tell them you've family coming."

"So has everyone else. Oh, come on, Katie!"

He tried to put his arm around me, but I ducked out of the way, dreading the thought of greeting Tom and Lisa on my own. I hardly knew them! Simon, being so good with people, would have broken the ice.

The atmosphere was electric, yet here I was acting like a grumpy Scrooge

Then I paused. They were Simon's family, for heaven's sake! Was I really such a wimp that I couldn't face them alone? However, I was still cross.

Plonking a pile of gaudy trimmings in front of Simon, I pointed at the ceiling. Ladders and I had never been compatible.

"And we need to go back to the supermarket," I announced.

****

Later, with David Essex crooning *A Winter's Tale* from the speakers, we traipsed around the busy store, hardly speaking.

I selected mince pies, Turkish Delight, pigs in blankets – all the while dodging parents in Christmas jumpers and their excited offspring. The atmosphere was electric, yet here I was acting like a bad-tempered Scrooge.

Christmas is all about children, Katie, I told myself sternly, and Simon wants to help give some disadvantaged kids a good time. Guiltily, I smiled at him.

"Simon, we need a tree and lots of fairy lights!"

I grabbed his hand and squeezed it. He smiled back and I sighed with relief. I couldn't bear it when we were not a hundred per cent together.

Later, Simon dutifully carted an artificial tree to the car and, once home, put it up straight away.

I raided Mum's box again, then stood back.

"Beautiful!" I said, as multicoloured lights lit up the room. "They'll love it!"

Even Bertie blinked, showing interest for a few minutes.

On Christmas Eve, after Simon left for work, I tackled Tom's old room – which was to be Lisa and Tom's bedroom during their stay – removing pot plants, the ironing board and bags of cat litter.

Most of it ended up in the shed. Then I fiddled with the tree again, adding yet more glitter, and giggling when Bertie tried to grab at the hanging lights with his paw.

Just before lunchtime I sat down with a coffee, wondering what I'd forgotten.

kitchen. I was about to go up to change when I remembered something else. Crackers!

"You can't have Christmas without crackers, Mum!" my son used to say every year, when he was little.

I grabbed my jacket. That supermarket was becoming my second home.

After picking up a box of luxury red-and-gold crackers, I wandered through the clothes department and found a rather fetching blue shirt for Simon and a sparkly red top for myself.

I felt quite smug. Lisa and Tom were going to be so impressed!

****

When I got home I let myself in, but stopped suddenly at the lounge door.

Facing me was a massive blur of green, stretching right across the coffee table amid a sea of clutter and debris.

Shattered baubles, strewn ornaments . . . the Christmas tree was down! Bertie – the culprit – was nowhere to be seen.

From the settee, my silver fairy, wand in pieces, beamed angelically up at me

Presents! I'd intended to get vouchers for Tom and Lisa yesterday, but weren't vouchers a bit boring?

Well, I had just finished a picture. A vivid experiment, that one: three children running through a field, lots of greens and purples.

I'd aimed for a painting that exploded with life and fun. Would Lisa like it? Probably not.

My mobile rang. It was Tom.

"Katie, we're going to be very late, at least another hour. Sorry, stuck in traffic!"

I told him not to worry, we'd have a late lunch, and rang off.

The ham salad was ready in the

I let out a long moan. From the settee, my silver fairy, wand in pieces, beamed angelically up at me.

After some wrestling, I managed to get the tree upright again, but I was back to square one regarding the mess. Unbelievable!

Then the doorbell rang. Dreams of calmly welcoming our guests to my new tidy house in my new Christmas top vanished. The reality was very different.

In old jeans and cardi, my hair a tangled mess, I was too shocked to give Tom and Lisa any more than half-hearted hugs.

I led them into the lounge, wincing ›

at the horror on Lisa's face as she stood there in her beautiful black overcoat.

"I'm so sorry. The cat knocked the tree down while I was out –"

"Wow!" Tom exclaimed. "Let's give you a hand."

"Not now," I said hurriedly. "Lunch is ready. You must be starving!"

As we began the meal, the back door slammed. Simon was back. I allowed myself to relax slightly.

"I managed to get away early. Happy Christmas, kids! Great to see you! How's life?"

"Fine, thanks." Lisa smiled, helping herself to salad.

"It's so good of you both to have us at short notice."

Feeling – and looking – as though I'd been through a wringer, I half-smiled, then frowned at Simon.

"Bertie's brought the tree down and it's chaos in the other room. No, leave it now," I added wearily, as Simon made a move to the lounge.

"But where is your cat?" Lisa put in anxiously. "Is he OK? I love cats."

Ah, something positive among the turmoil, I thought, as I answered.

"Bertie will have bolted into the garden. I'll fetch him later."

But neither of them were really listening. Tom interrupted me.

"We have something to tell you."

He glanced at his wife. "Lisa?"

I looked at her. She seemed quite embarrassed.

"I'm pregnant," she said. "You're going to be grandparents!"

Simon shouted his congratulations, then hugged Lisa while I just sat, numb.

Wonderful news! And even more wonderful was Lisa calling us both grandparents.

I felt choked up.

"Congratulations!" I managed. "A magical Christmas present!"

Father and son turned to each other, joking about sleepless nights, and I chatted to Lisa.

After the meal, Simon and Tom went out to fetch luggage from Tom's car.

There was an awkward silence in the room.

I tried to imagine Lisa coping with all the baby paraphernalia in her spotless minimalist haven. No doubt she would be the perfect mother.

"Katie, is it silly to be scared? I daren't tell Tom, but how will I cope?"

Then I realised she was frowning anxiously at me.

"Katie, is it silly to be scared? I daren't tell Tom, but how will I cope? I wish my mum was still alive . . ." She broke off.

I blinked. This was a very different Lisa. Impulsively, I put my arm around her.

"But you'll have us."

"Your son was really lucky, Katie."

"Eh?"

"Having such an easy-going, creative mum, I mean. I'm much too practical."

"You'll be fine, I promise! We all cope in our different ways."

As I spoke, I thought of the mess in the lounge and how little things like that mattered. Then about the picture I was giving Lisa tomorrow.

Whether she liked it or not, it was the thought that counted – coming, as it did, with all our love.

And Lisa could always hang it in the baby's room.

By Barbara Dynes

Smokin' Pork Meatballs

Ingredients (Serves 4)

- **375g pork sausagemeat**
- **100g cooking chorizo, minced or finely chopped**
- **1tbsp smoked paprika**
- **50g dry breadcrumbs**
- **Salt and freshly ground pepper**
- **2tbsp vegetable oil**
- **1 onion, peeled and sliced**
- **1 large yellow pepper, deseeded and sliced**
- **700g garlic passata**
- **150g frozen green beans**

1 Mix the sausagemeat, chorizo, 1½tsp paprika, breadcrumbs and seasoning together. Shape into 16 balls. Cover and chill for 30 minutes.

2 Heat the oil a large frying pan and cook the sausage balls, turning, for 10 minutes until browned all over and the juices start to run. Remove from the pan using a draining spoon and set aside.

3 Heat the pan juices and stir fry the onion and pepper for 2 minutes. Lower the heat, cover the pan and cook for 20 minutes until softened.

4 Stir in the passata, frozen beans and remaining paprika bring to the boil, then add the sausage balls. Cover and simmer gently for 15 minutes until hot. Serve from the pan with parsley and crusty bread.

RECIPES AND FOOD STYLING: KATHRYN HAWKINS
PHOTOGRAPHY: STUART MACGREGOR

Christmas Windows

An old, magical workshop sparks Emily's imagination but can she really bring a Christmas dream to life?

Emily stared up at an empty shop front. The Tudor-style façade stood four storeys high, squashed between a cafe and a boutique, its chimney disappearing into dismal, grey sky.

The windows were clouded with dust, and lettering that once spelled out 'Family Department Store' had faded above the shop's high doors. An estate agent's SOLD sign arched out beside it.

"I expect they'll turn it into flats."

Emily spun round. "Sorry?"

"Whoever's bought it." An elderly man leaning on a tartan shopping trolley pointed to the empty windows.

"My parents would take me shopping there every Christmas when I was a boy, to pick out a present from the children's department.

"The family who owned it used to decorate it lovely, they did. Holly garlands and big red bows outside; fairy lights, beautiful displays for show. It looked like a Christmas card come to life."

Emily smiled. "It sounds wonderful."

"It was." The man nodded, his eyes resting on the building for a moment.

"We all missed it when they shut their doors, decades back. It was the heart of this town, especially at Christmas. Those shop windows lit up like magic."

Emily's gaze flickered with emotion. Her eyes slid to the abandoned panes, the SOLD sign looming over her. A rush of anxiety swooped through her stomach.

Taking a breath, she exhaled and said, "You never know, maybe they will again."

"Ha!" The old man sniffed, pushing off on his shopping trolley. "Now that would be a Christmas miracle."

Emily's smile faded. Had finding Mary's old tin car just driven her to making a huge and costly mistake?

****

The garage workshop at the back of Mistletoe Cottage was, quite frankly, a mess. Drawings of machinery; oil cans; books; springs and random bits and pieces littered the floor, shelves, bags and boxes surrounding Mary's work bench.

"It was the heart of this town. Those shop windows lit up like magic"

"It looks like a mad professor's shed," said Jack, his excited eyes scanning the place.

Emily smiled at her eight-year-old's appraisal of his great great aunt's workspace. "She was a bit eccentric."

"A bit?" Sophie, her 12-year-old ›

PICTURES: DCT

daughter, held up an age-mottled, crumpled drawing labelled, "Time machine". Sketches of steampipes, springs, nuts and bolts swirled around it as though about to take off.

"OK, very eccentric," laughed Emily, her hands brushing across dusty paint tins and screwdrivers. "That's probably why she achieved so much in her life. She followed her dreams."

"She would affectionately call me, Uncle Peter and Harry her little elf helpers when we were trying to put together her latest invention in here."

Emily smiled, joyful memories spinning past her eyes like a carousel.

"Mary invented toys for all the big department stores and toyshops; toys which started out as squiggles and scribbles in this workshop."

"That's probably why she achieved so much. She followed her dreams"

Tears filled Emily's eyes, remembering how her parents would bring her and her brother, Peter, to stay with Mary for the Christmas holidays. Such happy times, running around the snowy garden with their scruffy dog, Harry, before piling into the workshop with Peter, their parents and Great Uncle Tom for a demonstration of Mary's latest invention.

It was hard to accept she was no longer here. "Mary was a trailblazer."

"What did she do?" Jack picked a wooden clown from a shelf, wiping the dust on his sleeve to reveal a wind-up key among its fabric costume. Turning it, Jack balanced the clown on the workbench and it started juggling teacups on wires.

"You've almost answered your own question there, Jack," said Emily, winding the key. The clown lifted its hat and bowed; tinny cheers echoing from within.

The trio laughed.

"Mary was a very clever and wonderful woman. She was a highly regarded toymaker, back in her day."

Jack's face lit up. "Like Father Christmas?"

"Don't you mean, Mary Christmas," said Sophie, grinning. "She did live in Mistletoe Cottage!"

They laughed.

"That's so cool!" Sophie leafed through an old sketchbook, her imagination sparked by the drawings and names.

Sophie's favourite subject at school was design and technology.

"Imagine earning a living selling toys!"

Emily could imagine. "I know! When I was your age, it was my dream to run a big shop. I would collect up things around your granny and grandpa's house, setting them out on the dining table next to a tiny cash register I'd been gifted for a birthday. Granny, Grandpa and Uncle Peter would play along, pretending to be my customers."

"Why didn't you follow your dream, Mum?"

Sophie's question caught Emily by surprise. She stared at a drawing on the workshop wall. It was of Harry, Mary's distinctive hand capturing the mischievous sparkle in their gone but much-beloved dog's furry face.

Why hadn't Emily followed her dream? Because she never believed it was a possibility? Emily's eyes slid to meet her daughter's gaze.

"I did," said Emily, wrapping her arms around her children's shoulders warmly.

"My other dream was to have two amazing children and I definitely got that!"

Sophie and Jack giggled, squeezing Emily's waist.

"Did Mary have children?" asked Jack.

Emily was silent for a moment. She'd spotted a tin racing car in a corner of the workshop, covered in cobwebs and thick, grey dust, but you could still make out the number 25 painted in red on the car's green bonnet. Four small tyres and a steering wheel had been crafted from wood, as had the dashboard inside. It was big enough for a small child to sit in.

Emily stepped towards it and crouched down, her hand polishing the racing car's number. "No, Mary didn't meet her husband, Tom, until later in life, too late to have children, but I know she would have been an incredible mum, and Tom an amazing dad."

Sophie's hands flailed in the air, excitedly. "Or you could buy your own shop, Mum, and follow your dream!"

Emily hesitated. Follow her dream. Mary would certainly approve of that idea.

Emily turned back to the dusty tin car, a picture of something magical forming in her mind's eye: bright colours; upbeat music; floors of happy faces browsing beautiful displays, she'd know her customers by first name!

No. That was a silly idea.

Though, what was that saying? Better to try and fail, than to never try at all.

Emily wanted her children to believe they could achieve their own dreams; just like Mary had wanted her toys to ignite the imaginations of the children who received them.

What was that saying? Better to try and fail, than to never try at all

"So, that's why Mary left her house and workshop to us and Uncle Peter?"

Emily looked at Sophie.

"Mary thought of Peter and I as the grandchildren she didn't have."

"Are we going to live here with Uncle Peter, Auntie Lauren and the twins?" asked Jack, mesmerised by the wind-up clown as it juggled the teacups again.

Emily chuckled. "No, Jack. I think Mistletoe Cottage might be a bit small for two families to live in. The cottage will be sold, and the money split between me and Uncle Peter."

"What are you going to spend the money on, Mum?" Sophie gazed at the tin car; her imagination already revving with ideas of how to make a matching motorcycle and sidecar.

Emily shrugged.

"I'm not sure yet. It would certainly pay off the mortgage on our house."

The future pilot flying a wooden aeroplane through their house; the future entertainers performing to friends from a box of magic tricks; the future scientists setting out their potion bottles in the garden shed...

****

Emily fell in love with the store as soon as she set eyes on it.

In the centre of a bustling town, it was the perfect setting for her dream shop.

As the estate agent showed Emily, Sophie and Jack around, Emily's heart skipped a beat with every creaky floorboard and glimpse of original wooden counter and display drawers.

The next couple of months were a frenzy of excitement, stress and fun. With a team of family, friends and builders, Emily transformed the shell into the most beautiful toyshop she could dream of and › by the December opening day, she could hardly believe what she was seeing as she walked the four floors.

Toys lined the Christmassy festive displays: a bookshop on one floor; planes, ships and trains whirling through another; a science room; an art space; giant numbers and puzzles; a junior haberdashery; a workshop. Emily even hired theatre performers, magicians and a face painter to celebrate their Christmas Grand Opening. She'd never felt prouder.

****

A crowd gathered outside the shop. The Tudor-style façade stood four storeys high, its chimney disappearing into a magical, snowy sky. The windows were shrouded with red velvet curtains, and lettering that now spelled out Mistletoe's Toyshop above the shop's high doors, Mary's sketch of Harry the new logo.

Emily, Sophie and Jack stood behind a large ribbon bow in front of the toyshop's entrance, a pair of scissors in hand.

"Three, two, one..." shouted the crowd. Emily, Sophie and Jack cut the ribbon together: "We proudly declare Mistletoe's Toyshop open!"

The curtains drew back in the windows, wowing the onlookers with a dazzling festive display. Toys, books and decorations had been imaginatively curated among stars of twinkling lights and Mary's original inventions.

The crowd cheered, pouring through the doors as snowflakes started to fall on their shoulders and woolly hats.

Happiness fizzed through Emily's heart, watching Sophie and Jack running into the shop with the crowds. Emily knew she had a lot of hard work ahead of her, but with the support of her family and a desire to succeed, she knew together they would make a success of it.

She suddenly spotted a familiar old man with a tartan shopping trolley wheeling through the crowd towards her, a young boy skipping alongside.

"You never said it was you who bought it," he said to Emily, pointing towards the toyshop's windows.

Emily smiled. "I couldn't quite believe I had, and wasn't sure I would be able to create a shop like this."

"It brings happy back memories," said the old man, taking in the magical windows and door arch of fir branches and grand decorations.

He patted the boy's shoulder. "Christmas miracles do happen!"

He patted the boy's shoulder; they shared the same grin and bright eyes. "Christmas miracles do happen!"

Emily glanced at Mary's tin racing car taking centre stage in a window display, the red number 25 and green bonnet shining beneath festive fairy lights.

"You know, I really believe they do."

Looking at the man and boy, Emily nodded to the toyshop. "Would you like to take a look around–?"

"Stanley," said the old man, smiling back. "My name's Stanley, and this is my grandson, Sam."

Sam grinned at her, his excited eyes darting towards the toyshop doors.

Emily's face sparkled with happiness. With a flourish of her hand, she said, "Welcome to Mistletoe's Toyshop, Stanley and Sam, and a very merry Christmas to you both!"

By Lisa Allen

A Successful Resolution

IMAGES: DCT

This new year would be different – now it was up to Tess to choose how she would fill her time . . .

Tess was reluctant to refer to them as New Year's resolutions, but there was undoubtedly something about the start of the year that made her want to make plans and lists to tackle in the months ahead.

That new diary tucked inside her handbag, the blank calendar hanging on the wall, twelve new months to fill . . .

This year would be a bit different, of course. Tess had retired from her busy job in the local hospital; her youngest child had joined his brother and moved away to go to university; and her mother was now living in a sheltered housing complex and seemed to have found a whole new life for herself.

All of which left Tess with more time to herself than she'd had in quite a while. This could be either a good or a bad thing – but on a positive note, it felt to her like the ideal time to come up with some resolutions.

She decided to do it properly with a paper and pen, and a cup of tea to accompany her thoughts.

The house was unnaturally quiet, though she imagined that, going forward, silence would be its normal state.

No more boys chasing each other up and down the stairs, no more games of indoor football – there had been so many of those over the years, despite Tess's pleas for them to take the ball into the garden! – and no more busy, noisy mealtimes.

"It might be nice, having the place to ourselves again," Joe had said, just after the madness of Christmas, once everyone had gone back to their respective homes.

And there was no denying that Tess enjoyed having peace and quiet to read, or knit, or just to think. But would the novelty of this wear off?

Which is why the resolutions could be useful. A clear list of things to do, giving her something to focus on in the year ahead. Nothing too drastic or life-changing, but enough to fill some of those spare hours.

Tess took a sip of her tea and nibbled her biscuit. Then, without further procrastination, she picked up the pen.

She pictured herself becoming slim and toned, walking more gracefully

She wrote *Tess's Resolutions* and a number one on the blank page, followed by *Learn a new language.*

How hard could it be? After all, millions of people across the world spoke more than one language and they couldn't all be geniuses!

Tess had always fancied learning to speak Italian – such a beautiful, musical language – and she felt sure she could make a start this year.

She'd get a "teach yourself" book out of the library, and maybe download an app on her phone.

Next on the list, Tess wrote, *Take up Pilates or yoga.*

To be honest, she didn't really understand the difference between the two – were they in fact the same thing? – and consequently wasn't sure which ›

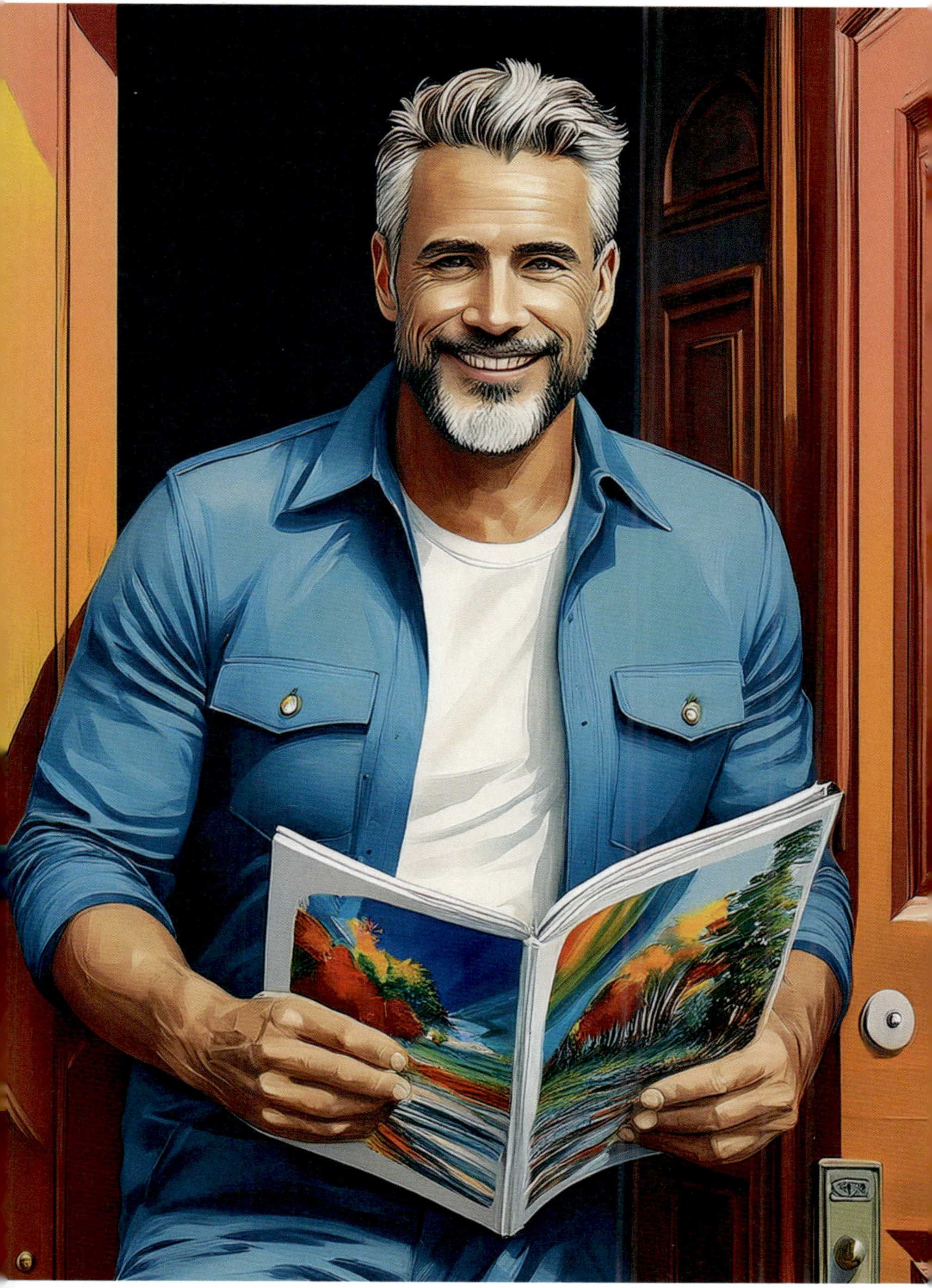

one she wanted to take up, but she could do a bit more research on that.

She pictured herself becoming slim and toned, sitting up straighter and walking more gracefully – Tess normally clumped from room to room.

She wasn't certain which type of exercise programme would best help her to achieve this. However, whatever she picked would surely be beneficial, she reasoned.

Or she could simply join whichever of the classes offered locally was on at the most convenient time.

She helped herself to another biscuit, feeling pleased with her resolutions so far. Perhaps one more?

Visit a new location abroad.

Tess had always loved travelling, so it surprised her to realise at this stage in her life how few countries she had managed to visit.

Resolving to go somewhere new left her with multiple options – apart from camping holidays in France and a few cheap-and-cheerful hotel breaks in Spain with Joe and the boys, Tess hadn't ventured very far at all.

She was in a rut, that was the problem. She had allowed herself to become bogged down with work, family, bills, the house and a million other humdrum everyday things, leaving very little space for bigger adventures.

****

Just then, she heard the front door open and close, followed by feet stamping on the mat. She looked up as Joe came into the room, smiling at her as he took off his jacket.

"It's freezing out there!" he said. "Nice and cosy in here, though."

He glanced across at Tess as he went to put the kettle on.

"Are you working on your New Year's resolutions?" he asked, noticing her pen and paper.

Tess smiled.

"Yep, I've got some great plans for the year ahead."

Joe nodded.

"Me too! For our silver wedding anniversary in April, for example."

He rummaged in his backpack and produced a glossy travel brochure.

It was all about a luxury retreat on the Sicilian coast which offered a variety of activities for guests.

Tess looked up at her husband in astonishment. "Joe, this is amazing!"

There were Italian language classes, yoga, Pilates . . .

Tess looked up at her husband in astonishment.

"Joe, this is amazing! I'd love to go to Sicily and, even better, a holiday here would tick off all my New Year's resolutions in one go! It's just as if you read my mind."

He shook his head and laughed.

"I didn't need to – you do realise you've had the same three resolutions for about the last twenty years?"

Tess laughed.

"Fine, I admit it," she said. "Now we just need to find a way to help you run a marathon, get a six-pack and learn how to play chess."

After all, she wasn't the only one who struggled with New Year's resolutions.

By Marie Penman

Lebkuchen

Ingredients (Makes 30)

- **200g runny honey**
- **80g butter**
- **200g plain flour**
- **1tsp baking powder**
- **½tsp bicarbonate of soda**
- **2tsp cocoa powder**
- **2tsp ground ginger**
- **1tsp ground cinnamon**
- **1tsp grated nutmeg**
- **½tsp allspice**
- **125g ground almonds**
- **25g dark brown muscovado sugar**
- **25g mixed peel, very finely chopped**

For the icing

- **100g icing sugar**
- **1tbsp hot water**
- **1tbsp lemon juice**

For the chocolate finish

- **100g melted plain chocolate**

1 Line two baking trays with non-stick baking paper. Place the honey and butter in a saucepan and heat gently, stirring until the butter melts. Set aside to cool.

2 Sift the flour, baking powder, bicarbonate of soda and cocoa into a large bowl. Stir in the spices, ground almonds and sugar. Add the chopped peel and stir in the honey and butter. Knead gently to a dough. Wrap in cling film and chill for 30-45 minutes until cold and firm.

3 Preheat oven to 180°C, 160°C fan oven, Gas Mark 4. On a lightly floured surface roll out the dough to a 1cm thickness and cut out rounds, stars, hearts or shapes of your choice, using a pastry cutter. Place on the prepared trays and bake for 15-16 minutes until slightly risen and firm.

4 Leave the biscuits to cool for 2-3 minutes then transfer to a wire rack. If coating with icing, mix together the icing sugar, water and lemon juice and dip or brush over the biscuits while still warm. It will set as they cool. If coating in chocolate, leave until cold then dip in the melted chocolate. Leave to set.

RECIPES AND STYLING: JENNIE SHAPTER
PHOTOGRAPHY: JON WHITTAKER

Each Week For You To Enjoy
My Weekly
Your Feel Good Read
Amazing Cookery
Favourite Celebrities
Up-to-date Health News
Fabulous Fiction
PLUS
◆ Puzzles ◆ Fashion ◆ Beauty ◆ Real Life
You'll Love It!
On Sale Every Tuesday
PICTURE: SHUTTERSTOCK

Brain Boosters SOLUTIONS

SUDOKO FROM PAGE 17

1	2	5	4	9	8	7	3	6
7	4	3	1	2	6	9	5	8
9	8	6	5	3	7	2	1	4
2	6	1	8	5	9	4	7	3
3	7	9	6	4	2	1	8	5
4	5	8	7	1	3	6	2	9
8	9	4	2	7	5	3	6	1
5	1	7	3	6	4	8	9	2
6	3	2	9	8	1	5	4	7

CODEWORD FROM PAGE 21

Phrase: THE CLEANER

O	P	P	R	E	S	S		S	P	I	N	A	C	H
	E		E		W		I		A		Y		H	
G	R	E	G		I	N	T	E	R		L	E	E	K
	V		R		P		A		A		O		V	
H	A	R	E	B	E	L	L		M	A	N	T	R	A
	D		T				I		O				O	
T	E	X	T		A	C	C	O	U	N	T	A	N	T
			E		L				N		R			
Q	U	A	D	R	U	P	L	E	T		A	J	A	R
	K				M		O				P		G	
M	U	E	S	L	I		S	K	E	L	E	T	O	N
	L		C		N		I		N		Z		N	
M	E	N	U		I	N	N	E	R		I	R	I	S
	L		F		U		G		O		U		S	
P	E	R	F	U	M	E		P	L	U	M	B	E	D

WORD WHEEL FROM PAGE 17 The nine-letter word is PLUMMETED

KRISS KROSS FROM PAGE 39

G	H	E	T	T	O		B	I	O	P	S	Y
	Y		E		V		E		C		U	
I	D	L	E	N	E	S	S		H	Y	P	E
	R		N		R		O		R		E	
N	O	V	A		S	Y	M	M	E	T	R	Y
	E		G		E						N	
A	L	L	E	G	E		S	E	P	T	U	M
	E						E		R		M	
E	C	S	T	A	T	I	C		O	B	E	Y
	T		O		E		L		V		R	
C	R	A	W		N	A	U	T	I	C	A	L
	I		E		E		D		S		R	
O	C	E	L	O	T		E	P	O	N	Y	M

SUDOKO FROM PAGE 55

4	3	9	2	6	1	7	8	5
8	5	2	9	3	7	1	6	4
6	1	7	5	8	4	2	3	9
7	8	1	3	4	9	5	2	6
3	4	5	8	2	6	9	7	1
2	9	6	7	1	5	8	4	3
1	2	3	6	9	8	4	5	7
9	7	8	4	5	3	6	1	2
5	6	4	1	7	2	3	9	8

WORD WHEEL FROM PAGE 55 The nine-letter word is FINANCIER

CODEWORD FROM PAGE 61

Phrase: LES MISERABLES

S	U	R	E	S	T		S	Q	U	E	L	C	H	
L		E		E		S		U		X		O		F
O	S	T	R	A	C	I	S	E		E	N	R	O	L
P		R		B		L		S		M		G		A
P	E	A	C	O	C	K		T	O	P	P	I	N	G
Y		C		R		W				T				G
	S	T	U	N		O	A	T	H		T	W	E	E
W		E		E		R		U		A		O		D
A	I	D	E		A	M	E	N		M	I	M	E	
L				S				G		B		A		J
T	H	A	N	K	E	D		S	T	R	A	N	G	E
Z		L		I		R		T		O		H		T
E	L	F	I	N		O	V	E	R	S	H	O	O	T
D		I		N		L		N		I		O		E
	R	E	C	Y	C	L	E		C	A	N	D	I	D

KRISS KROSS FROM PAGE 72

C	R	I	T	I	C		A	R	M	F	U	L
	E		R		H		T		I		N	
B	I	G	A	M	I	S	T		N	A	A	N
	N		G		P		A		I		D	
I	S	L	E		P	A	R	A	M	O	U	R
	T		D		E						L	
S	A	W	Y	E	R		B	O	U	N	T	Y
	T						A		N		E	
D	E	S	I	G	N	E	R		D	A	R	T
	M		N		I		R		R		A	
H	E	R	D		N	O	I	S	E	T	T	E
	N		I		N		E		S		E	
S	T	E	E	L	Y		R	E	S	I	D	E

Brain Boosters SOLUTIONS

SUDOKO FROM PAGE 73

1	8	9	6	7	2	3	5	4
4	3	5	9	1	8	2	7	6
2	7	6	5	3	4	9	8	1
6	5	2	8	9	7	4	1	3
8	4	1	3	5	6	7	2	9
7	9	3	4	2	1	5	6	8
3	6	4	2	8	5	1	9	7
9	2	7	1	6	3	8	4	5
5	1	8	7	4	9	6	3	2

CODEWORD FROM PAGE 81

Phrase: EMMA RADUCANU

■	S	K	I	L	F	U	L	L	Y	■	S	A	G	A
Q	■	I	■	O	■	S	■	O	■	S	■	B	■	C
U	N	L	I	T	■	E	L	B	O	W	■	A	R	C
E	■	L	■	U	■	D	■	■	■	E	■	N	■	I
U	N	J	U	S	T	■	S	H	R	E	D	D	E	D
E	■	O	■	■	■	S	■	O	■	T	■	O	■	E
■	D	Y	E	D	■	K	A	T	I	E	■	N	A	N
O	■	■	■	O	■	I	■	T	■	S	■	■	■	T
V	I	A	■	W	A	I	V	E	■	T	U	S	K	■
E	■	B	■	N	■	N	■	R	■	■	■	O	■	O
R	E	D	E	S	I	G	N	■	S	W	I	P	E	D
S	■	O	■	I	■	■	■	H	■	R	■	R	■	D
E	L	M	■	Z	E	B	R	A	■	I	R	A	T	E
L	■	E	■	E	■	I	■	L	■	N	■	N	■	R
L	A	N	D	■	S	T	R	O	N	G	B	O	X	■

WORD WHEEL FROM PAGE 73 The nine-letter word is COMPONENT

KRISS KROSS FROM PAGE 87

S	K	E	T	C	H	Y		M	E	T	A	L
P		N		U		A	D	O		H		A
O	U	T	F	L	O	W		H	E	R	O	N
O		O		L		L	E	A		O		T
R	O	M	P		A			I	O	N		E
		B	L	E	N	D	E	R		E	A	R
H			Y		T		P		R			N
A	S	S		D	E	M	I	G	O	D		
B		W	H	O			C		B	E	A	M
I		A		R	O	T		C		D		O
T	O	T	E	M		U	N	E	Q	U	A	L
A		H		E	L	F		D		C		A
T	H	E	I	R		T	W	E	E	T	E	R

SUDOKO FROM PAGE 93

1	2	6	4	7	9	8	3	5
8	9	5	6	3	2	1	7	4
7	4	3	5	1	8	9	2	6
3	6	1	2	9	4	5	8	7
5	8	2	3	6	7	4	9	1
9	7	4	1	8	5	3	6	2
6	3	7	9	4	1	2	5	8
2	1	8	7	5	3	6	4	9
4	5	9	8	2	6	7	1	3

WORD WHEEL FROM PAGE 93 The nine-letter word is DECREMENT

CODEWORD FROM PAGE 96

Phrase: RUN, FATBOY, RUN

A	S	K	A	N	C	E	■	W	I	N	D	I	N	G
■	Q	■	B	■	Y	■	O	■	N	■	A	■	U	■
A	U	R	A	■	C	R	U	S	T	■	V	E	R	B
■	A	■	S	■	L	■	T	■	E	■	I	■	T	■
C	L	U	E	L	E	S	S	■	R	A	D	I	U	S
■	L	■	M	■	■	■	E	■	J	■	■	■	R	■
L	Y	R	E	■	E	N	T	R	E	N	C	H	E	D
■	■	■	N	■	X	■	■	■	C	■	A	■	■	■
P	O	S	T	S	C	R	I	P	T	■	S	H	A	H
■	R	■	■	■	E	■	N	■	■	■	H	■	M	■
H	I	C	C	U	P	■	B	I	B	L	I	C	A	L
■	F	■	L	■	T	■	R	■	A	■	E	■	Z	■
K	I	L	O	■	I	D	E	A	L	■	R	U	I	N
■	C	■	C	■	O	■	D	■	S	■	E	■	N	■
W	E	E	K	E	N	D	■	B	A	N	D	A	G	E

KRISS KROSS FROM PAGE 97

R	U	S	S	E	T		S	T	E	P	P	E
	N		C		W		O		T		E	
F	I	S	H	B	O	W	L		H	A	R	E
	N		E		S		V		E		S	
I	T	E	M		O	V	E	R	R	I	P	E
	E		E		M						I	
E	N	T	R	E	E		U	N	P	I	C	K
	T						T		R		A	
M	I	G	R	A	I	N	E		O	R	C	A
	O		O		N		N		S		I	
S	N	O	W		T	E	S	T	A	T	O	R
	A		D		E		I		I		U	
P	L	A	Y	E	R		L	O	C	U	S	T

SUDOKO FROM PAGE 101

5	2	6	4	3	8	1	9	7
9	1	8	7	2	6	5	4	3
3	4	7	1	5	9	6	2	8
2	7	5	3	1	4	8	6	9
6	8	4	5	9	2	7	3	1
1	9	3	6	8	7	4	5	2
4	6	9	8	7	3	2	1	5
7	3	1	2	6	5	9	8	4
8	5	2	9	4	1	3	7	6

CODEWORD FROM PAGE 109

Phrase: BADGER SWAGGER

	P	A	N	G		P	O	U	R		F	L	A	K
P		V		I		E		N		S		O		A
A	C	O	R	N		R		A	R	C	H	W	A	Y
C		C		S	Q	U	I	B		A				A
K	N	A	V	E		S		A	I	R	L	O	C	K
A		D		N		E		T		C		U		
G	R	O	G	G	Y		M	E	M	E	N	T	O	
E			U			E		D			I			B
	C	O	N	T	E	X	T		L	E	T	H	A	L
		W		R		P		J		N		E		I
B	E	L	I	E	V	E		E		F	E	A	S	T
R				N		C	U	R	I	O		L		Z
I	L	L	I	C	I	T		S		R	A	I	S	E
A		A		H		E		E		C		N		D
N	E	W	S		I	D	L	Y		E	D	G	Y	

WORD WHEEL FROM PAGE 101 The nine-letter word is **PRIMITIVE**

KRISS KROSS, P123

V	I	S	I	B	L	E		O	A	S	I	S
E		I		O		S	I	R		P		U
R	O	L	L	M	O	P		A	T	L	A	S
S		I		B		Y	E	N		I		P
O	R	C	A		B			G	I	N		E
		A	P	P	E	A	S	E		T	O	N
A			T		A		E		G			D
B	I	D		F	U	N	E	R	A	L		
O		A	G	A			P		L	I	S	T
L		M		V	I	M		P		M		R
I	M	A	G	O		E	C	L	I	P	S	E
S		S		U	R	N		E		I		N
H	I	K	E	R		U	N	A	I	D	E	D

SUDOKO FROM P131

5	6	1	7	4	3	2	9	8
7	8	4	6	9	2	5	1	3
2	9	3	8	5	1	6	4	7
4	7	6	5	3	9	1	8	2
8	1	5	2	6	7	9	3	4
9	3	2	1	8	4	7	6	5
6	2	8	4	1	5	3	7	9
1	5	9	3	7	8	4	2	6
3	4	7	9	2	6	8	5	1

CODEWORD FROM P135

Phrase: LE GAVROCHE

B	E	R	S	E	R	K		E	Q	U	I	N	O	X
	L		T		I		L		U		G		V	
V	E	T	O		G	U	A	V	A		L	E	E	K
	V		C		H		R		R		O		R	
B	A	S	K	E	T	R	Y		T	H	O	R	A	X
	T		R				N		E				W	
M	E	M	O		L	U	X	U	R	I	A	T	E	D
			O		I				L		R			
C	H	E	M	I	C	A	L	L	Y		C	A	S	H
	O				E		I				H		E	
G	O	R	D	O	N		M	A	R	Z	I	P	A	N
	D		O		S		P		A		T		S	
F	L	O	G		I	D	L	E	D		E	D	I	T
	U		M		N		Y		I		C		D	
E	M	B	A	R	G	O		J	O	S	T	L	E	D

WORD WHEEL FROM PAGE 131 The nine-letter word is **LACQUERED**

KRISS KROSS, P141

U	N	L	E	S	S		B	E	S	I	D	E
	E		L		H		A		T		I	
B	I	G	A	M	O	U	S		O	A	S	T
	G		S		W		I		O		A	
T	H	A	T		E	S	C	A	L	O	P	E
	B		I		R						P	
T	O	U	C	H	Y		S	U	R	F	E	R
	U						U		E		A	
G	R	A	N	D	S	O	N		T	I	R	E
	H		I		T		B		R		A	
C	O	V	E		O	B	E	D	I	E	N	T
	O		C		A		A		A		C	
A	D	V	E	R	T		M	A	L	L	E	T

SUDOKO FROM P147

9	1	4	5	3	2	6	7	8
8	2	5	6	7	9	4	1	3
7	3	6	8	1	4	2	9	5
1	5	7	9	2	3	8	4	6
2	9	8	4	6	5	7	3	1
4	6	3	7	8	1	9	5	2
5	7	2	1	4	6	3	8	9
3	8	1	2	9	7	5	6	4
6	4	9	3	5	8	1	2	7

KRISS KROSS, P153

S	C	E	N	I	C		B	A	S	Q	U	E
	O		O		A		O		A		N	
U	N	L	I	S	T	E	D		B	A	I	L
	T		S		H		G		L		N	
K	E	T	O		O	P	E	R	E	T	T	A
	M		M		D						E	
S	P	H	E	R	E		A	L	P	I	N	E
	L						C		A		T	
C	A	T	H	O	L	I	C		R	A	I	L
	T		A		A		L		S		O	
G	I	R	L		T	R	A	M	L	I	N	E
	V		V		C		I		E		A	
S	E	R	A	P	H		M	A	Y	F	L	Y

WORD WHEEL FROM PAGE 147 The nine-letter word is **THEREFORE**